ANGELINE

ANGELINE

A Novel

ALLEN MCCUNE

iUniverse, Inc.
New York Lincoln Shanghai

Angeline

iUniverse books may be ordered through booksellers or by contacting:

iUniverse
2021 Pine Lake Road, Suite 100
Lincoln, NE 68512
www.iuniverse.com
1-800-Authors (1-800-288-4677)

ISBN: 978-0-595-44173-0 (pbk)
ISBN: 978-0-595-88505-3 (ebk)

Printed in the United States of America

PART I

1

A shovel breaks the hard ground. It hollows and mounds the split earth in regular time, one measure by one. A man digs on a lonely hilltop under a winter sky and a tree stripped of its leaves. He labors on, wiry and strong, his gray face furrowed and worn.

I step under the bare branches and stand among the stark knotted roots, hunting shelter out of the wind. There is none to be had, and raising the collar of my overcoat I look on in the silence as he works, breath smoking gray in the slanting gray light.

The Greeks recognized an underground god. God of secrets and wealth, all the subterranean powers. They saw him as grim, invisible, ruling over ghosts and the dead. Unlucky even to mention his name. A realm so gloomy they believed him beyond love. In that underworld though his word was final.

It had hardly been four months since the stock crash. The company was still strong and had not yet begun closing operations or laying off. There was still work for a man who knew his way below ground.

Some of them allowed that God would not follow a man underground. Or that there were two gods, one above and one below. That it was the lower power who ruled underneath, with his own commandments and laws.

When somebody got sick with influenza and died, or lost a child, or had their foot crushed by a coal car, they would ask me if it was part of God's plan. I told them that it was, that they suffered for a deeper purpose. I am not sure anymore. Now I wonder, and in my heart suspect that any design lying behind this world is not subject to human decipherment.

There was this old boy up there one time with his right fist caught in a collapse, crushed under about a ton of rock. They brought me underneath to try and keep him still until they could pry him loose. I could hear him screaming down at the end of the tunnel. By the time I got to him, he was trying to cut off his hand at the wrist with a pocketknife.

2

When he woke up she was already in the kitchen. It was still dark. The wind was blowing the bare branches against the windowpanes. He could hear the river. It was swollen with spring melt, sighing in its bed. A few night lamps were shining through the trees. On the other side of the river the bank was wild and uninhabited.

John Black sat up in bed and lit a cigarette. He smoked in the silence, tapping his ashes in the cut glass ashtray on the bedside table. The smell of biscuits and coffee moved into the room through the dark house. He finished smoking and pushed the glowing stub into the glass.

The washroom floor was cold and he shaved with cold water. He primed the razor on the strop and splashed the water against his face. The cold made him breathe in sharp and quick through his teeth. He lathered his face and shaved half-awake. He rinsed off the soap and combed his hair down wet handed. A shirt and overalls hung on the back of the door and he dressed and went out shivering.

It was warm in the kitchen. The fire in the stove shed the smell of cedar kindling. Warm light shone from a lamp on a shelf above the counter. A white china plate and napkin were set at the table and he sat down and breathed in the coffee and biscuit smell. Angeline stood by the stove in the glow of the lamp. He watched her pale arms moving in the warm light, her slim figure shifting under her apron.

She brought the pot over from the stove and poured coffee into his cup. He drank it hot and black. She lingered there a moment by his chair watching him absently. She touched the back of his hair. Then she moved back into the warm aura of the stove.

He took out the pack and lit a cigarette and sat smoking mute under a gray halo. When the biscuits were done she brought them hot out of the stove and shook them into a basket. She set them on the table with a plate of salted butter. The biscuits steamed golden in the lamplight. There were potatoes on the stove frying in an iron skillet. He drank coffee and smoked and rubbed his eyes and woke up the rest of the way.

She fried an egg in the pan with the potatoes and brought it over and filled his plate. He let the cigarette sit in a notch on the ashtray while he ate. The smoke rose in a thin column by the window. He took two biscuits and buttered them and ate the egg on one of them as a sandwich. She came over and poured more coffee into his cup and poured herself a cup. She stood leaning against the counter and watched him eat.

She had gone into the back room when he wiped up the last egg yellow with a biscuit and got up from the table. He took the tin dinner bucket and thermos from where she had left them ready on the counter and went wordlessly out of the kitchen and down the hall. His cap was on a chair by the door. Still the only light shone from the kitchen. He stopped inside the door in the dark hallway and pulled on his coat. He stood for a moment and listened back into the stillness of the house. Then he picked up the lunchpail and went out.

Outside the sky was still dark. He closed the screen door behind him and came down off the porch and started walking. A dog came from somewhere out of the dark and followed him down the road. Black shadows of houses stood silent against the charcoal-colored sky.

Beyond the houses gray shapes gathered along the tracks. Men were sullen and bleary eyed. They crouched in the gravel and smoked, holding their caps, their dinner buckets littering the ground.

When he approached they only turned and nodded in the dark. One of them said his name and again fell silent. John set his gear on the ground and stood and looked down the tracks, the rails curving away parallel under the road. Up along the ridge he could see the flash of headlights. The company trucks started coming before dawn.

At the camp Daniel came down off one of the other trucks. He fell in alongside John and the brothers walked together without speaking. John glanced back at the younger man. Wild dark hair and a ruddy stubble of beard. Daniel looked up and managed a sleepy grin.

Behind the mountain the sky was lit with the first faint glow neither blue nor gray. Clouds hung there like columns of pale bone. Men filed toward the hole in silence. Together the brothers crossed over the threshold into the dark.

Human shapes moved down the shaft in silhouette, backlit by the faint light of dawn. One by one their hat lamps began to flash on. The beams stabbed into the dark and lit the iridescent black surfaces of the tunnel. John struck the flint and ignited the carbide lamp on his cap. The acetylene flame left a faint whiff of phosphorus.

Daniel was already gone when John turned down a different passage, following the other shadows. He could hear and smell the mules before he saw them. They gave out a close rooty odor, wheezing and straining with the weight of the cars. He could hear them braying down the gallery. Powder hung in the dank atmosphere and he could taste the bad air. The hole was noise, dust, flickering light and shadow. Cries echoed down the tunnels.

He followed a train of empties half a mile down into the low coal. The cars hit a switch and turned behind the mule and disappeared in the dark. He headed straight on. The fire boss was still down there, crouched against the mineral, checking the fissures for damps. He nodded to the man, passed him by and went even lower.

Now the only light was from his own lamp. He had to lean down hard to get through, his tools scraping along the ground. A side passage was barred across, the word FIRE written on a sign above it. He moved beyond, further into the dark. They had laid a new piece of track up to his patch. He crossed into the last chamber and set his things under the wall. He went along in the dark and checked to make sure the props were right. Then he started to drill.

He worked hard all morning, hand drilling and tamping powder and shoveling the blasted coal. He loaded three tons before noon and pulled back to leave something for after lunch. At break he went up and dipped water out of the barrel and drank and washed some of the dust off his hands. He took off his cap and pushed his hair back. Men were settling along the wall under the timbers. He sat down beyond them on the edge of the gallery.

He lifted out the tray from the lunchpail. Fishing down in the bottom he felt the hard-boiled eggs sitting in the cool water. He took the eggs out and tipped the pail up and drank the water out of the bottom. Then he peeled the eggs and ate them. They had the faintest taste of sulfur. In the tray there were biscuits and cold chicken wrapped in wax paper. He ate everything and drank black coffee out of the thermos.

At first light David stood in front of the mirror and dressed. He studied his own features in the glass, dark and lean and clean-shaven. Pressed white shirts hung on the back of the door. He took one down and put it on and knotted a silk tie around his neck.

When he came downstairs he found the newspaper folded on the dining room table next to a plate of poached eggs and toast. He sat and drank coffee and looked at the front page. Sarah came out of the kitchen with a small glass of hand-squeezed orange juice and set it on the table in front of him. She went on into the hall. He heard the front door and she came back through the dining room with the milk bottle and went back in the kitchen without a word.

He finished eating and folded the paper half-read and got up and put on his suit jacket. She came out to the front hall and helped him with his overcoat. He told her goodbye and took his valise and hat and went out the door.

The car came up around the side of the mountain and crested the gravel road running down into the camp. The sky steel-colored behind the trees. David slowed at the guard post and waved to the men in the shack huddled over a stove with heavy overcoats and shotguns. They waved him through and he passed by the foreman's tiny house. He pulled up in front of the company office and parked along the walk. Down the hollow he could see the empty trucks by the road and the mouth of the mine gaping black and the dead silver of the tracks running into the dark of the tunnel.

The blinds were lowered and the afternoon sun slanted through, cut into thin horizontal strips dividing the room into staggered registers of dark and light. Joe shut the door of the superintendent's office behind him and came and stood over the desk. David leaned forward in his chair and watched him unfurl a cylinder of drawings. Joe spread them out on the desk under the green-shaded lamp. He pointed to an obscure area beyond the maze of tunnels that continued amorphous and unbounded off the page. He traced the region's edge with his fingertip.

"It stretches out here under a ledge of brittle slate," Joe said. "Goes just about straight down. How far we can't say."

He glanced at David. "According to the engineers, there looks to be some amount of coal there. No safe method of getting to it though."

David put his glasses on and studied the paper. "How much mineral are we talking about?"

"A seam this breadth is likely to hold as much coal as all our other live operations together."

David looked at him. "What's the risk?"

"Fairly high, I'd say. We may be able to get at it by a different road, but it may take us six months or more of hard blasting."

David studied the map for a long moment. Then he looked up at Joe again.

"I don't know," he said. "You tell them I'm going to have to consider it."

3

Long shadows cast down from the mountain already darkened the camp when the miners emerged. The sky was a sheet of lead stretched above them. The breath of the men hit the late winter air steaming as they filed out into the final hour of daylight. Along the road the trucks were pulling up in a ragged caravan. John found his brother among the men, sullen and blackened like charred wood. They walked out together tired and silent, their overalls stiffened with grit. He found a place in the bed of the truck and set down his things and pulled Daniel up after him. They sat waiting for the truck to fill up. John smoked dumbly and offered his brother the pack.

When they came down off the truck at the tracks he left Daniel at the crossroads and started down the hill into town. The dog found him coming up the road and followed him through the yard and up onto the porch. He took off his boots and socks and swept black dust off his overalls and from his hair. He left his lunchpail and cap and boots on the porch and stepped inside the screen door. He opened the door and called into the house but he knew she would be out back.

When he came out onto the back porch toward the garden he had on a faded red flannel shirt and dungarees clean of coal dust. He held his moccasins in his hand and walked down the steps into the grass barefoot. The loose dust had been combed out of his hair, his face and hands washed clean except for the black grit driven under his nails. His pallid face showed against the shadow of the house. The sun was down in the trees, sending its last shafts horizontal and broken through the evergreen branches. The garden sloped down from the house toward the black screen of branches along the bank. Behind it ran the swollen brown line of the river.

Angeline was kneeling at the edge of the garden pulling up a few pale shoots of weeds. She had not noticed him come out of the house. He stopped in the grass and watched her. She stood up, one fist clutching the thin weeds, clotted dirt still clinging to the roots. She wiped her forehead with her free hand. Her chestnut hair was tied back, falling brown and gold in wisps along her neck. The wisps caught the failing light behind her, casting her in a honeyed glow. Her faded blue cotton dress fit her close, showing the slim lines of her limbs and the curve and fullness of her body.

John came forward in the grass. She turned and saw him. Her eyes lit up and her full mouth and easy smile made him smile in return. He went down to the edge of the garden. They stood together in the cooling dusk.

"Daniel may appear later this evening," he said. "Maybe for supper."

"All right."

John took her pale hand and rubbed the dirt away and held it in his callused fist. He could smell the wet ground and the sweet rich odor of compost. His fingers found the smooth metal of the gold ring and lingered there.

He brought a harrow out of the shed and they started to work. He would turn a piece of ground and she moved along the furrow and spread compost from a bucket and seeded cabbage and early collards from her apron pockets. They worked until the sun quit completely and they were only two shadows under a sky luminous with a few early stars and the moon's stolen light.

John leaned back in the zinc washtub grinning with his knees up out of the water. Angeline came in from the kitchen with a smoking kettle. She poured the hot water into the tub and he sat up quick and lifted his naked body up out of the water.

"Hooo!"

"Hold your horses there," she said.

"Whew—"

He lowered himself gradually back down in the tub, the water steaming around his body. His hair stuck out in spikes of cemented coal dust and bathwater.

"I like your hairdo."

"I thought I might wear it to bed this way," he said, grinning up at her. "Like a wild animal."

"No sir, you won't."

She knelt by the tub and washed him with a rough sponge, scrubbing his arms and hands to remove the coal dust. She washed his back and neck and rubbed his muscles. The radio played some faint hillbilly tune in the other room.

He stood up nude in the spent water, his body smoking in the cold air of the washroom. She unfurled a big white towel and wrapped him in it with her arms around him. She lingered there pressed against his bare wet back, feeling the warmth of it on her face and her body and darkening her dress and apron with water. After a long moment she let go and went back into the other room. John stepped out of the water and dried himself. He could hear her in the kitchen singing a little song to herself like a nursery rhyme.

There was a little man
And he had a little gun
His bullets were made of
Lead, lead, lead

He went to the brook
To shoot a little duck
Shot him right in the
Head, head, head

Take him home
To my wife Joan
Make me a fire, wife
Make, make, make

Make me a fire, wife
To cook my duck
While I go back for the
Drake, drake, drake

After supper they sat in the parlor on the hearth in front of the fire. Angeline sat on the rug with her legs tucked under her and her apron still over her dress. She leaned back against her husband, letting herself be held. John had one arm wrapped around her shoulders and smoked with his free hand, tapping his ashes on the bricks of the hearth. Daniel stood out in front of them in the middle of the darkened room, lit only by the red orange glow of the stove coals.

"I was up on Big Cliff," Daniel said. "Hunting ginseng and toadstools. It was just at sundown and my pouch was near full, and I stopped out by the rocks at the edge of the trees over by the lookout. I was just sitting there, staring out at the valley and listening, and then it struck me that everything had gone still. No birdcalls or crickets whatsoever. Not a sound."

He paused and looked askance in the silence.

"So I look back in the trees and there she is. She could smell me but I knew she couldn't see me too good. Otherwise she'd have come straight on. She just shambled up a few steps—"

He slouched forward imitating the animal's movement.

"—and sniffed my air. Then she started talking to me—"

He made fierce bearlike noises, plaintive barking roars with the rhythm and intonation of human speech.

"Warning me I guess that she was a damn sight meaner bear than she thought I was. Well, I about nearly shit when I heard that and I started backing down off the cliff—And they say never do run from a bear, but right then I couldn't remember what exactly it is that they say—"

"I expect not—"

"So I start running full tilt down the side of the mountain, toadstools be damned, and here she comes after me, maddern hell. So then I completely lost my sense and started hollering anything I could think of to get her to quit—"

"The hell you say—"

They broke out laughing and Daniel grinned in the firelight and kept acting out the scene.

"Oh that was swift—"

"Just yelling my head off like a damn fool and the whole time getting tore all to hell on my arms and face and toadstools and ginseng spilling out all down the side of the mountain—"

John grinned up at his brother and took a drag on the stub of his smoke. He drew Angeline back against himself, and they sat like that the rest of the night, leaning together on the hearth in front of the stove with Daniel out in the dark room standing up and acting things out, making them all laugh and then sitting down again on the rug grinning, his face lit up with the glow from the embers of the dying fire.

4

David stood alone on the porch in his shirtsleeves, suspenders down from his shoulders. The sun had already gone behind the mountains and he looked out over the valley in the grainy twilight. Beyond the town the river ran cold and dark. Along deserted streets lamps gradually winked on in the windows of houses. The only sounds were dogs barking somewhere far off and the faint cries of children coming in for the night. Behind everything was the whisper of the river.

He loosened the silk tie knotted around his neck and undid the first shirt button at his collar. Sarah came up the hall and stood at the screen door.

"Supper's ready."

"All right," he said. "I'll be there directly."

He came inside. In the dining room was a single place laid out at the head of the table. He looked into the kitchen.

"Why don't you come on and sit down and have supper with me?"

"Oh no, I've already had too much," she said. "I'm just going to clean up in here."

He sat down and she came back carrying a dish with pot holders and served him from it. He ate a supper of roast beef with stewed potato, carrot and onion and nearly drained the bottle of claret that stood decanted on the table. He left the plate of meat unfinished and poured a final glass of wine. He leaned back in his chair and stared at the candle flame and out the dining room window into the dark beyond. After a while she came in and began clearing the table. She looked at his plate.

"You didn't like it."

"That's not it," he said. "You just gave me a helping that was a bit overgenerous."

"All right then."

She took the plates and disappeared back into the kitchen.

After supper he went into the parlor and took a cigar from the cedar humidor on the mantel. He clipped it with a knife he took out of his pocket and lit it and stood smoking by the fireplace. In the corner on a table draped with a lace square was a framed photograph of a young woman. She was smiling and her hair was drawn back from her face. The white line of her neck showed against a dark background.

He came home from Princeton when the old man died. Took over the mine and the store for the company and took to the job well. In some other towns along the river there was always some shooting or carrying on. Men jailed over debt to the company. He always seemed to use his sense though and cut a man a fair deal.

He always had brandy and real bourbon bootlegged from Kentucky. Caribbean cigars. Good opera disks from Charleston that he played on the victrola. He was a hand at chess. I learned the European openings by studying him. We got on.

Both of us partial to the classics. There never was an excess of conversation though.

He could type one hundred words in a minute. Read Latin and Greek. I was aware of a few pieces of verse he had published in some of the magazines. Lost a wife to the grippe. That was before I came here.

I drove up the road along the tracks and in the headlights I could see the house standing back along the woods. I turned down the gravel drive and pulled along the house. The car died and I turned off the lights and got out and came up the walk onto the porch and rang the bell. Sarah came to the door and welcomed me. She took my coat and hat in the front hall and hung them in the closet. She told me to go on in the parlor and I thanked her. I stepped through the sliding double doors that stood open and into the low-lit room.

David was sitting on the brick hearth, his profile dark against the ruddy glow of the fire. He turned and saw me and smiled, his face lean and handsome. His dark hair shone in the dancing light. The room was shadowed and masculine with lamps shedding warm light in several corners. He stood up from the hearth and smiled and came over and shook my hand. The board was already set up in front of the fireplace on a low marble top table flanked by two leather armchairs.

I sat down behind white and he said he always liked the way the ivory pieces showed against my black shirt and suit coat. Sarah came in with a tray of ice and soda. Whiskey in a crystal decanter. She set everything down on the end table and went out of the room. A moment later stepped in the doorway wearing her coat.

"I'm going to go on now."

"All right. Thank you, Sarah."

"I'll see you in the morning," she said. She looked at me. "Good night, Father."

"Good night, Sarah," I said. "Thank you."

She went out and we heard the door close and turned back to the board.

"Now, let's see here—"

I opened and as we exchanged moves I played swift and fluid, hoping I might disarm my opponent with confidence.

"Whoa there, have you been studying manuals behind my back?"

I grinned and looked down at the board, putting on a mock-serious tone.

"And he put his hand in his bag, and took thence a stone, and slang it, and smote the Philistine in his forehead—"

"Is that legal, using scripture to win at chess?"

"Don't try to change the subject to theology," I said.

I looked up at him and we both grinned.

He got up from his chair behind the board.

"Can I build you a drink, Nathan?"

"I don't see why not."

"All right then."

He went over and made two bourbon and sodas while I studied the board. He leaned over the table and handed me the glass and sat down again. I took a drink and the whiskey vapors kindled an amber flame in my chest and behind my eyes.

We played three games and he won the last two. In the final game he flanked my phalanx of pawns and drove the white king out from his cover and the game was decided well before it ended. We drank several more bourbon and sodas as we played. After I conceded the last game I got up and went to the hall closet. I came back with a small leather-bound book from the pocket of my overcoat.

We sat by the fire with worn editions of Greek plays spread out on our laps. As he thumbed the pages I could see in the margins of his dog-eared copy innumerable notes, questions, definitions and references hand-scrawled in pencil over numerous readings. We took up where we had left off on some other night, taking turns reciting the Greek and offering our own translations, working slowly but confident in our reading. We stopped to discuss the meanings of obscure words and unusual scansion or to offer some exegesis of the action itself. A train passed by in the night and ran down the valley along the river. Its horn faded into the distance as David assayed a chorus, his voice clear and rhythmic.

Man the master, ingenious past all measure
past all dreams, the skills within his grasp—
he forges on now to destruction
now again to greatness.
When he weaves in
the law of the land and the justice of the gods
that binds his oaths together

he and his city rise high—
but the city casts out
that man who weds himself to inhumanity
thanks to reckless daring.
Never share my hearth
never think my thoughts, whoever does such things

It was past midnight when we finished. The fire had burned down to embers and the ice and soda were gone and the whiskey half gone. We stood at the front door and I put my coat on and we shook hands. We were both feeling good with whiskey and I put on a mock-serious tone.

"My son, I haven't seen you at church in some time," I said. "Day after tomorrow I expect to see you at early Mass."

"Yes, Father."

We both grinned and I turned and went out the door. I waved back and walked off into the night and he held up his hand in farewell. He turned and went inside and closed the door behind him.

He shut off the porch light and the lamp in the hall. The house was empty. He climbed the stairs in the dark and followed the path of lamplight into the bedroom. He looked at the clock. He sat down on the edge of the bed and took off his shoes. He rubbed his face and stared into the empty room. The clock kept ticking in the silence.

The hospital ward stretched long and white, a line of high windows along one wall. The afternoon light fell across the polished white floor and the empty beds. The air tasted faintly of bleach. A folding partition divided the room and I stepped past it and saw that he was awake. He looked up and tried to smile. I could hear the rasp of his ruined lungs.

"Hello, Will."

"Father—"

"How have you been getting along?"

"Not too bad. They won't let me smoke though."

"I believe your smoking days might be over."

"You're more than likely right."

The nurse brought a chair and set it behind the screen. I unbuttoned my coat and sat down by the side of the bed. He followed me with his eyes without any other movement except the labored rise and fall of his breathing. His face was the color of stove ash. He did not look at all well.

"The superintendent sends his regards," I said. "I know he's been meaning to come up here and see you."

"That aint necessary. You tell him he's already done enough. He's a good man. Tell him thanks again for me."

"No problem."

I reached in my coat pocket and took out a few envelopes.

"I brought you some mail," I said.

I put the letters down on the low steel table beside the bed. He smiled and took a breath as if he were going to say something but he fell into a coughing fit. It turned into a violent wheezing hack. The sound echoed down the ward. It was nearly a minute before it subsided back into the regular shallow rasp of silicosis. He closed his eyes and sank back in the bed.

"I'm going to die, Father."

"That's not what I heard, Will. They told me you're holding steady."

For a moment he lay still, his eyes closed. Then he opened his eyes and looked off into the room.

"There aint no cure for black lung," he said finally.

I watched him. I didn't say anything.

He looked at me and nearly managed a smile.

"It's all right," he said. "I thought about it. I aint afraid no more."

That night I went back up to the superintendent's house. It was rare for us to play more than once in a week, but I was glad for the company. We sat by the fire concentrating on the game in silence, barely into our first drink. Somewhere off in the dark there was a crack.

"Was that a shot?"

"Sounded like," David said.

He got up and looked out the window but there was nothing outside the glow of the porch light. He stood there for a minute looking and then he saw a shadow moving across the field. A woman was coming up through the yard toward the house.

"It's Mary Beth Summers," he said.

He left the window and went into the hall and opened the front door. I came out after him and stopped in the doorway. Mary Beth was standing there, whimpering. Her face shone with tears in the porch light. She was almost hysterical.

"Ed's been shot—"

"What happened?"

"Oh God, he's shot and I don't know what to do—"

Sarah came into the hall from the kitchen. She saw that Mary Beth was crying and she put her arms around her. David turned and went upstairs and came down a minute later with a shotgun.

"I'm going over there," he said.

"I'm coming with you."

I started after him toward the door. He stopped and turned back to the two women in the hall.

"Sarah, call Dr. Perry. Tell him to come up to Ed Summers' place right now. Somebody's been shot."

We left the house and started across the field in the dark. A line of small houses ran along the road at the edge of town. We moved toward the nearest one. There was a light on in the front room. We went up on the porch and peered in the window but the curtains were drawn. David stood and listened at the door holding the shotgun.

"Is anybody there?"

There was a silence. Then a bleak voice called out.

"In here," it said.

David went in with the shotgun and I followed. A lamp in the corner shed sickly yellow light. Ed was sitting back on the ragged sofa with his leg stretched out in front of him. His face was ashen in the lamplight. The right leg of his trousers was soaked in blood from the knee down. Blood thickened and pooled on the rug in a dark puddle under his leg. The burnt taste of gunpowder hung in the air.

"Judas priest, Ed—what happened?"

"What the hell does it look like? I'm shot."

There was an old thirty-eight caliber pistol on the end table under the lamp. David breeched the shotgun and unloaded the shells and put them in his pocket. He laid the gun down inside the front door along the baseboard. He took the pistol off the table and opened the chamber and checked it in the light. There were five more rounds in the cylinder and he tilted the pistol back. The lead slugs slid out and disappeared into his hand.

I went into the kitchen and came back with a towel. I knelt at the foot of the couch and tied it taut under his knee as a tourniquet. He shut his eyes and sucked air through his teeth. The rag was immediately heavy and wet with the blood that had already soaked through his clothes, but the wound looked like it had nearly staunched itself. My hands were dark and sticky with his blood. It smelled metallic and vaguely sweet. Kneeling down on the rug I could taste the corn whiskey coming off his acrid breath. A drained mason jar lay overturned on the floor.

The women had come across the field after us and were standing on the porch in the doorway. Ed's wife had one of Sarah's shawls wrapped around her shoulders. David stood in the middle of the room and looked at him.

"Who shot you, Ed?"

"Shot myself."

"How in the hell did you manage that?"

"I was cleaning my gun."

"You shot yourself in the back of the calf while you were cleaning your gun?"

"That's right."

"Is that what happened, Mary Beth?"

David turned and looked at her. She was watching her husband with a pitiful look on her face. He sat there breathing heavy through his nostrils.

"Mary Beth?"

Looking desperate, she nodded yes.

Ed shifted on the couch, grimacing.

"Goddamn it," he said.

"What's wrong?"

"It hurts like hell," he said.

An hour later we stood waiting on the front porch. Dr. Perry came out the screen door with his bag and the three of us stood there under the porch light. David spoke to him in a low voice.

"How does it look?"

"He's all right," the doctor said. "Just a little upset. He's not going to be working for a while though."

"Someday one of those two is going to kill the other one."

David looked at Dr. Perry. "Would you let me have the bill for this, Cy?"

"If that's what you want. No problem."

"Thanks for coming up here at this hour."

"Glad to help," the doctor said. "I'm going to go on now."

"All right. Thanks again."

We both shook hands with the doctor and watched him walk out to his car and pull away. Sarah came out of the screen door with the folded shawl. David touched her arm.

"How is he doing?"

"He's already asleep."

"Is she going to be all right?"

"I think so," she said. She shook her head. "These people."

"Let me go in for a minute and say goodbye," I said.

I went back into the house. She was in the front room down on her hands and knees with a rag and bucket, sopping up the blood. She stopped and looked up at me.

"Is there anything I can do for you right now?"

"No, Father. Thank you. We'll be all right."

"I'll come back in a day or two to see how you are."

"All right," she said.

When I came back out they were waiting in the yard. The three of us walked back toward the house across the field in the dark. The house stood there stark and white in the porch light. When we came in the door Sarah went into the back of the house.

David looked at me. "Wait here a second," he said.

"All right."

He turned and went up the stairs. I took my coat out of the hall closet and put it on and stood waiting at the front door. He came down the stairs holding an envelope. He handed it to me.

"Here's fifty dollars," he said. "Could I ask you to give them ten dollars a week out of this?"

I looked at him. "I could do that," I said.

"When they ask you who it's from you might say there was a church collection."

"I'll say an anonymous friend."

"All right," he said. "Good."

5

The shadow of the stone cross slanted in the yard and families in Sunday clothes, faces scrubbed and hair combed down, filed through the doors into the rustic church. Sun streamed through panels of stained glass, casting pools of blue, gold, and deep rose over the floorboards and across the shoulders and pale faces of the congregation. Dust motes hung suspended in shafts of sunlight. People settled along the pews and silent children stared up fascinated at scenes of the betrayal, trial, and scourging of the Lord.

The organist worked the pedals in the low, shadowed balcony. An acolyte lit the candles on the altar with a brass rod and I stepped out of the vestry and moved along the rail onto the dais. At the altar I knelt and crossed myself under the images of the saints. The other servers in their white robes came up and stood behind me facing the altar. I rose and turned, looking back into the room. The last few people were coming in from the yard. The deacon closed the door behind them and started back down along the aisle.

The door opened a final time and I saw David come in. He touched the low font. He knelt and genuflected. The chords of the organ rose to the climax. People were already sitting. David moved along the back of the church. I acknowledged him with a glance. The organ swelled and stopped and the congregation knelt. I began the Mass.

In nomine Patris, et Filii, et Spiritus Sancti—

David took off his hat and sat along the outer aisle in the last pew near the door. He knelt and bowed his head.

Judica me, Deus—

An acolyte stood on the dais gently swaying the lit censer. The perfumed smoke drifted out into the air. The dusky sweet odor of the incense, the heat from the coal stove in the back of the church, and the warm human smell of the congregation all combined in a lethargic wave through the room.

Quare me repulisti, et quare tristis incedo, dum affligit me inimicus?

David raised his head and looked down along the pews. There was a young woman sitting along the aisle in the middle of the congregation. She turned her head and her face caught the light coming through the high windows.

Quia peccavi nimis cogitatione, verbo et opere—

He watched her silhouetted profile and the curve of her neck as she turned. She moved into the light. He looked at the line of her mouth and the almond shape of her eyes. She wore her hair pulled back with wisps of curl showing at her neck. She sat close by her husband.

Et clamor meus ad te veniat—

She seemed to feel him watching her and glanced back along the pews. For a moment he looked at her and then lowered his eyes.

I kissed the altar and rose and moved to the pulpit. I stood at the lectern, looking out over the congregation. The people rose and I opened the book and started to read.

I will greatly multiply thy sorrow and thy conception; in sorrow thou shalt bring forth children—

She stood in her pale dress with her head bowed and the sun coming down through the tall windows. The honey-colored down on her arms caught the glow. From the back of the room he watched her.

—in the sweat of thy face shalt thou eat bread, till thou return unto the ground; for out of it wast thou taken: for dust thou art, and into dust shalt thou return.

After the sermon and the creed the bell rang three times. The organ started again in the loft and the tabernacle was opened and the host brought out. With a sign I called the congregation forward for the body and the blood. People started to file down toward the altar rail. I stood waiting, flanked by servers holding the cup and plate. The organ wheezed on, filling up the room. Its hoarse music and the creaking of the ancient pews and floorboards under the shifting bodies and their warm, close breath were like the respiration of the church itself.

The fading light of dusk glowed in the windows of the study. Shadows lengthened and turned imperceptibly over the scarred oak surface of the desk where David worked. Ledgers lay open, spread out everywhere and buried under sheaves of paper lined with chicken scratch. He traced a column of figures down the page with the edge of his pen and reached the bottom and went back and checked it again. He set the pen down and leaned back in the chair. He stretched and took off his glasses and rubbed his eyes. He got up from the desk and walked out through the glass doors onto the balcony and stood at the wooden rail.

A blue silence had settled over the houses in the town below. A few yellow lamps gleamed along the darkening streets. The murmur of a car motor passed down the dirt road along the tracks. Its taillights flashed for a moment and then disappeared around the bend. It was still winter but for the first time the air was warm, tinged with the smell of thawing soil and the scent of the river moving fast with runoff from the warming hills. The first green tips of early buds were only just beginning to force themselves out of the bare branches and the sap to flow again in the dormant bodies of trees.

He stood out in the faint breeze in his shirtsleeves and watched the slate-colored dusk. In the bottom of the valley the river glittered and coursed in the final hour of light. He stood a moment longer, then stepped back into the room. He put on his jacket and went out into the hall and down the stairs. He came out onto the porch and let the screen door close silently behind him and came down the front steps and started walking out across the field.

Angeline stepped out of the screen door onto the back porch with a basket of clean damp laundry. She came down the cinderblock steps into the yard and set the basket down in the thin grass. There was a wire suspended from the corner of the house to the shed along the edge of the barren garden. She dug in her dress pockets and started to hang the sheets and towels with wooden clothespins. When she had emptied the basket she took it back to the house and set it on the steps. She untied her apron and folded it. She draped it over the side of the basket and walked out to the edge of the garden plot.

She stood and looked over the dark and warming ground. She smelled the dusky odor of the soil. The air was warm for March and heavy and smelled of rain. The sky deep blue and luminous where the sun had been. She slipped out of her shoes and stood in the loam. It was strangely warm and loose as if it were already fully spring. She leaned down and absently pulled a few weeds.

She wandered barefoot across the yard and stood by the wire fence. At the edge of the woods the fragile white blossoms of bloodroot had appeared. She knelt in the grass and plucked a few of the pale flowers and lifted them to her face, closing her eyes and letting the petals brush lightly against her nose and her mouth. She stood up and put one of the small blossoms in her hair and started walking down the hill toward the river.

Overnight the willows had changed from gray to the pale yellow of their first bloom. She walked through the bare sycamores and found a path along the steep bank sloping down to the sand. The stones were cool and smooth under her bare feet. She looked across into the dark, tangled growth on the other side. A mist hovered in the trees. Water birds moved in vague silhouette down along the shadowed bank. The river made a faint rushing sound. The sun dropped along the line of the hills. A band of rose light still glinted out of the west, shifting on the water.

The breeze moved the surface of the river. The air felt warm against her bare arms and neck. She reached back and pulled the band away and let her hair fall down onto her shoulders. She stepped forward to the shallow edge. The cold water lapped against her ankles. She leaned down and with her cupped hands splashed water on her face and neck. It was cold and she breathed in deeply. The blood quickened under her warm skin.

She stood and listened. There was no sound except the river and her own movement in the shallows. She turned and looked around in the twilight, up and down the riverbank. She was completely isolated. She reached to her throat and silently unbuttoned the neck of her dress. She pulled the cloth away and leaned down again and splashed water on her bare shoulders.

The water was cold and bracing on her skin. She looked again in the deepening shadow down along the bank. The bare sycamore branches hung out over the water and there was no movement. She unbuttoned her dress the rest of the way and pulled it over her head. She stood barefoot in her white slip at the edge of the water. Her limbs were slim and white. Her breasts stood out under the thin cotton shift.

She folded the dress and left it draped over a branch and began to wade slowly down into the river. The water rose coldly over her thighs as she went deeper. She inhaled sharply from the cold and with a faint gasp pushed away from the bank. The water rippled soundlessly around her body as she swam out past the shallows.

The river was icy and swift with the thaw and her lungs filled deeply and her heart beat quickly with the chill. The cold braced her and she dove under and held her breath and came up. She looked out over the dark surface of the water. The sky was deep blue and the light almost gone. She turned and took a breath and started swimming back toward the bank.

She rose up out of the river and stood and wrung her hair over the stones. The wet slip clung to her body. The cold of the water began to fade and the warm breeze moved over her skin. She looked up and saw him standing at the edge of the trees. He was only a few feet away from her. He wore a dark suit and his face was pale against the shadowed undergrowth. She was startled but made no sound or movement.

In the dusk the curve of her body showed under the thin wet slip. David stood and looked at her, motionless under the trees. She was very beautiful. She straightened and met his gaze. She did not seem ashamed or afraid.

Then the sun fell in gold and red behind the mountains and lit the river. He watched her. The ruddy light flashed dyingly on the water. Her skin was very white, her dark hair clinging wetly to her neck. Her body moved with deep even breaths. She stood very still.

At that moment an extinct universe opened again inside him, blooming like a deep red flower, incarnate and warm. The nourishing blood rushed back, washing through the dry dead organ that nurses mute longings and wants, that watches like a visceral eye, as tender as a wound, perceiving beauty only, that aches and craves and feels the deep stabbing pain of beauty and loss that can never be apart, never separate.

6

David woke before the alarm. He sat up in bed and swung his legs out and leaned on the edge of the bed rubbing the sleep out of his eyes. He went into the bathroom and turned on the hot water and looked in the mirror for a moment until the glass steamed up and obscured his face. He shaved and washed and combed a drop of pomade into his hair and found a clean undershirt. Pressed shirts hung inside the closet door and he dressed and went downstairs.

There was coffee on the table and a plate of toast and poached eggs and the newspaper. He took the coffee cup and went out on the front porch. He stood against the rail and looked out over the town and across the valley at the veil of mist draped in rarefied layers along the dark flank of the mountain beyond the river.

At the end of the day David stood at the window of the office. He watched the miners come up the hill toward the waiting trucks. He saw the two brothers walking together with their gear slung over their shoulders, their heads leaning together as they talked. They climbed onto the truck bed and cleared a spot and sat together smoking cigarettes, waiting for the truck to fill up and haul them back down the hollow to town.

After work David went out to the woodshed behind the house and dug up a rusted old axe. He sat on a stump with an oilcan and a rag and rubbed off the rust on the dull blade until it shone clean and blue in the dusky light. He found an old whetstone worn concave and held it steady on his knee while he moved the axe head in tight circles over the stone until the edge showed a silver crescent against the dark blue metal.

The logs were still stacked under the eaves of the shed where he'd had them left in the fall. He found a battered handcart leaning in the shed and hauled a load over to a low broad stump. The light had already begun to fail when he started splitting wood but he worked on for an hour until his arms ached and his body strained with that single-minded aim as if he meant to clear his brain altogether of any other thought.

At twilight he came down through the trees and stood again at the water's edge. The banks stretched darkly on either side, the sky a deepening blue over the cleft of the river. He looked down along the bank across the rocks. The water beyond shimmered as the light broke across it in a million glittering scales.

He heard a sound behind him and turned. Angeline stood among the rocks in a pale gauzy shift. He stepped down the bank where she stood waiting. There was only the sound of the moving water. He took her hand and kissed it and held it against his lips. He pulled her to him and kissed her mouth. His hand found her breast and he knelt in the wet sand and pressed his face into her abdomen against the sheer wet material. He could feel her breathing hard against him, her heart beating and her hands buried in his hair and he pulled her down over him in the smooth flat stones and sand and pulled the slip down around her. He closed his eyes and he could smell the dusky salt smell of her skin.

He heard footsteps on the rocks. He opened his eyes and looked up. John stood over them, flushed and panting. With his left hand he jerked David's head back and then pushed the barrel of the pistol hard against his temple and cocked the hammer.

David opened his eyes. He sat up and breathed deeply and shook himself awake. He looked around the room. It was morning. Sunlight was streaming through the windows and he could smell coffee percolating in the kitchen downstairs. He got up and went to the closet still in his nightclothes.

From the bottom he pulled out the leather suitcase and laid it open on the unmade bed. He took several shirts down from the hangers and folded them carelessly and put them in the suitcase with his socks and undershorts and shaving kit and a spare suit. He fastened the bag and opened the drawer of the bedside table and found a leather wallet under some papers. He took money out and put it back in the drawer.

His breakfast was out when he came down and he set the suitcase in the hall and sat down at the table. Sarah came in from the kitchen with the pot and poured coffee into his cup. She looked into the hall and saw the suitcase.

"Where are you going?"

"I have to go into Charleston for a few days."

"Is everything all right?"

"Everything's fine. I just have to take care of some things. I don't expect to be gone long. Do you think you could look after the house?"

"Of course I will."

She looked at him for a moment and then left the room. He ate half the toast and one of the eggs and drank the coffee. He did not look at the paper. When he had finished he went into the parlor and picked up the receiver and dialed.

"Hello? Hey, Joe. No, everything's fine. Listen, I need to go into town for a few days. Family business. Yes. Just came up. I'll be back as soon as I can. Everything all right there? Good. Handle things for me while I'm gone. All right. Thanks, Joe. See you then."

He hung up the receiver and took the watch out of his pocket and looked at it. He went out in the hall and put on his overcoat and took his hat and picked up the suitcase.

Sarah stood in the kitchen doorway wiping her hands on her apron.

"I've already missed the C & O," he said. "I'll have to go down to the river and see if Mr. Platt will take me across to catch the Virginian."

She watched him. He turned absently back into the hallway.

"Thank you, Sarah. I'll see you in a couple of days."

"All right," she said. "I'll see you when you get back."

David came down the hill toward the river. He stopped at the bottom of the hill before the path went into the trees. A wooden pole stood there and suspended from it on a wire a steel chime. He set his bag down in the dust and took the rod and struck the metal tube. A deep metallic note rang out across the valley, hollow and clear and resonant in the morning stillness. He shaded his eyes and looked across the river to the far bank. After a few moments a figure came slowly down through of the trees to a rowboat at the water's edge. David picked up his suitcase and started walking down the path.

The sun was climbing over the hills, burning the last mist away from the surface of the water. He stood waiting along the rocks. By now he could see clearly the faded wooden hull and old man's back and his arms pulling the oars in slow deliberate ovals. As the boat neared the shore the man lifted the oars and pulled them up in the hull. The boat glided through the shallows and touched the riverbank with a faint scrape. David stepped down and gripped the bow and pulled the boat up on the sand.

"Morning, Mr. Platt," he said.

He wasn't sure whether the old man had heard him. Platt looked up and nodded gravely to him and reached a bony arm out to take his bag. David handed it over the bow and stepped widely into the boat and sat down in the stern. Mr. Platt took an oar and pushed them away from the bank. He sat down and fit the oars into the tarnished steel locks. The boat drifted into open water and he began turning the bow back toward the far shore. Mr. Platt rowed slowly and with effort. David watched him. His ancient face was lined with long vertical creases down his forehead and sunken cheeks. There were large sand-colored blotches on his gaunt hawklike nose.

When they reached the other side David helped him pull the rowboat up onto the bank. Mr. Platt tied the line to a cinderblock embedded in the mud. David paid the fare and thanked the old man. Platt disappeared up the path without looking back. David lifted his suitcase out of the boat and started walking up the slope toward the tracks.

There was no platform or station there only a flat bare patch at the foot of the hill along the rails. He waited in the silence. Soon the noise of the engine came somewhere distant around the bend of the mountain. The train's horn sounded out across the valley, sad and plangent. A moment later it appeared through the trees, already slowing itself to stop.

The engine passed him and pale wisps of steam swept around his legs. A passenger car slowed and came to a stop. The conductor leaned out of the door onto the metal stairs. David handed his bag up to him. The coal smoke smelled vaguely of sulfur.

The conductor took out a book of tickets and looked at David.

"Return?"

David looked up. "No return," he said.

"Suit yourself."

There were only a few people in the car. A porter took his suitcase and put it in the bin. David walked to the back and sat down by the window. The conductor started to move back through the car taking tickets. David felt the engine brakes turn loose and the car lurch forward. He looked out the window toward the town as the train pulled away. He watched the river valley unfold and the play of light on the water and the patterns of the first faint spring colors on the passing mountains.

7

David stepped past the doorman into the lobby of the hotel. It was cool and quiet in the long room. Plants stood in shadowed corners around low tables where men sat smoking cigars, the smoke curling under the glow of floor lamps. He walked up to the front desk carrying his suitcase with his overcoat folded on his arm. The desk clerk stepped toward him behind the counter.

"Good morning, sir."

"Hello," David said. "A balcony room if you have one."

"Do you have a reservation?"

"No, I don't."

"Let me see if there is something available."

The clerk looked down at the open ledger behind the counter.

"Your name, sir?"

"David Hansford."

"And how long will you be with us?"

"I don't know exactly. Just a few days I expect."

The clerk looked again at the registry and took a room key down from the wall behind him. He turned to a bellman standing by the elevator.

"Take this gentleman up to 1102," he said.

When they found the room the bellman unlocked the door and carried in the suitcase. David handed him a coin and the bellman thanked him. He gave him the key and left, closing the door behind him. David hung his hat and took off his suit jacket and laid it on the bed. He opened the door to the balcony and looked out over the street at the cars passing in the late morning sun.

In the afternoon he walked down the street with his hands in his pockets looking into shop windows. He went into a grill and sat down at the lunch counter. He ordered a cup of coffee and a steak done rare. They served it with french-cut potatoes and he pushed the fries around the bottom of the plate with his fork to soak up the gravy and the dark red juice of the meat. He sat and smoked and drank two more cups of coffee. He watched the man work the grill and listened to the sounds of glasses and silverware clinking and the deeper murmur of human voices.

He sat smoking at the lunch counter for almost an hour after he had eaten and the counterman had cleared his dishes. The lunch crowd had already thinned out and only a few people remained. He finished smoking and asked for the check and paid and went out. There were fewer people in the street and he wandered down toward the tall buildings.

He stopped in front of the big window of a department store. There was a display of women's fashions with female mannequins wearing dresses of the latest design, fur coats, and elegant hats.

He went inside through the revolving doors and looked absently around at the scarves and coats. Across the aisle there was a young woman standing behind the cosmetics counter. She was pretty with dark hair. She smiled at him and he smiled back uncertainly.

"Hello, sir."

"Hello."

He took a step toward the counter and saw that she was holding a bottle of perfume.

"Would you like to smell this one?"

She sprayed perfume on her wrist and held it out to him.

He took off his hat and leaned down, holding lightly the soft skin of her wrist. He closed his eyes and inhaled the perfume, lingering there a moment in that pose breathing deep the scent of roses and summer evenings and the dark sweet heavy smell of vegetation.

"It's very nice," he said, opening his eyes.

Men in dark suits and women in evening dresses stepped out of automobiles as they pulled up in front of the theater. A valet would come around and take the woman's hand as she emerged and then go around the car and slip behind the wheel and drive to the parking lot.

David stepped out of the dark of the sidewalk into the bright aura of the marquee and joined the crowd filing into the lobby. The name of the play was spelled in moveable letters on the illuminated panel under the permanent neon sign of the theater name, the *Atreus*.

A girl in a kiosk was checking coats. Ushers looked at tickets under the chandeliers and escorted couples down the aisles into the dark theater. He took a playbill from a young man standing at the door and looked at his ticket stub and stepped into the half-light of the dimmed chandeliers.

At intermission he smoked a cigarette in the lobby. Waiters moved through the room balancing trays of champagne glasses. He stood in the corner and watched the handsome and privileged people. There was a woman on the other side of the lobby with her back turned toward him. She was standing with another woman and two men. One of the men was smoking a cigarette and laughing.

The woman wore an elegant evening dress with her hair up in a style that showed the line of her neck and her white shoulders. Her necklace glittered under the chandeliers. Locks of her hair fell loose in dark ribbons. She turned her head slightly in conversation and he recognized her. It was Angeline. He started to walk across the room, hesitating at first and then more sure. He stopped just behind her and reached out and touched her shoulder.

"Miss?"

The woman turned around and faced him. She was lovely with dark features. It wasn't Angeline. She looked at him with a curious expression.

"I'm sorry," he said. "Excuse me."

He turned and walked out of the theater and down the darkened street.

The door to the balcony stood open. The room was dark except for the headlights of cars reflected up from the windows of the darkened building across the street. The lights would flash for a moment as the cars passed by in silence and then disappear. He sat at the edge of the bed in his shirtsleeves, staring straight ahead at nothing.

8

Dawn broke down the hollow as the men came off the trucks, walking the last hundred yards down the slope to the hole. It had turned cold overnight after an early thaw. Down the mountain the colors hung muted on the boughs. The ground was hard with frost and the cinders crunched under their boots. They came silent, bundled in their thin jackets and breathing smoke, their stubbled faces chapped in the sharp wind. They hurried down the slope, eager to get underground out of the sting. Up the hill at the company house they could see warm light burning in the windows.

The brothers crossed the threshold together out of the wind. Just inside the tunnel John stopped and looked at the younger man.

"See you tonight."

"All right," Daniel said.

John turned and started down the shaft. Daniel watched him disappear into the dark.

David sat at his desk writing under electric light. Dawn was still a pale glow in the windows. His pen scratched in the silence. He heard the door open and the sound of someone entering the outer room.

He got up and leaned out his office door and saw the secretary taking off her coat. She looked at him.

"When Joe comes in, ask him to come see me," he said.

He left the office door open and sat down again behind the desk and looked at some papers. After a little while Joe stood in the door.

"What's up?"

"Close the door and come on in," David said. "Have a seat."

Joe sat in a chair in front of the desk and waited. David watched him.

"How might we go about opening up that seam?"

Joe looked at him. He sat back in the chair and sighed and reflected a moment.

"You know we can open that vein from the other side of the hill," Joe said. "It would just be a matter of a few months of blasting. Are you sure you want to do this?"

"Yes, I am," David said. "And I'm asking your opinion on the logistics of it."

"Well, we might put together a temporary crew to do the setup. We'll have to ask for volunteers. I won't require a man to work a hole I'm not willing to work myself. We might pay a little extra."

"Absolutely," David said. He leaned forward slightly and looked at Joe. "In your mind, who might supervise an operation like this?"

"Well, there are a few," Joe said. "But again, it's going to have to be on a freewill basis. Otherwise, we'd be asking for a whole mess of problems."

"What about John Black?"

Joe looked at him. He considered a moment, then nodded.

"He knows how to dig coal for sure," Joe said.

Men filed out of the hole in a ragged column, exhausted and dark with dust like convicts locked a hundred years in some subterranean gaol. David stood at the window in the office watching through the drawn blinds as they emerged and headed for the trucks. He watched a moment longer, then stepped away and sat down behind the desk. Joe got up and looked out the window.

There was a knock and Joe stepped over and opened the door. John stood there with his lunch pail and cap, his overalls blackened by a day's work but his hands and face scrubbed clean. His hair was combed back out of his face. Joe shook hands with him and motioned him into the office. John acknowledged the superintendent with a polite nod.

"Come on in," Joe said. "Sit down, son."

John sat in the chair provided for him. Joe continued to stand. David watched them without expression.

"We called you in here because we're planning to open up a new trial operation," Joe said. "There's going to be a temporary crew put together and we'll be asking for volunteers. We wanted to know how you'd feel about acting as crew chief until it's opened up and stabilized, and a regular crew moved in."

There was a pause. They waited for his reaction. John sat attentive but his face remained blank. He glanced at the superintendent.

"It would mean better pay and good experience," Joe said, "but I'm not going to lie to you. It's not going to be easy. There are risks involved."

Joe paused. From behind the desk the superintendent watched John without expression.

"You talk it over with your family," Joe said. "You can give us your decision on Monday. Anyway, thanks for coming in."

John stood up and shook hands again with Joe.

"Thank you, sir," he said. "I appreciate it. I'll let you know."

He looked at the superintendent. David watched him. John nodded to him and turned and opened the door and went out. Joe closed the door behind him and turned and looked at David.

After work John found her out behind the house in the garden. He came down the slope past the shadow of the house and watched her. She knelt there with a trowel trying to break the hard ground by hand. The line of a blacksnake moved in the grass under the bare vines on the grape arbor.

She looked up and the declining sun shone in her face. She shaded her eyes with one hand. He crouched down on his haunches beside her. She turned back to her work.

"There aren't too many ways a man can make regular crew chief," he said. "Or foreman eventually. This is something for us."

"We get by," she said.

Her eyes stayed on her work. He watched her. For a long moment he didn't say anything.

"We're going to want to start a family sometime," he said finally.

She stopped digging and looked at him. "We are a family."

He stared at her a moment. Then he sighed and looked away.

"If I'm going to do this," he said, "I need to have my wife behind me."

He stood and started back up the slope. She still knelt there in the broken earth. She watched him walk up to the house and disappear inside.

It was dark and the brothers sat in the woods on the hull of a fallen tree. They could see every star through the black branches above, stripped bare except the first early buds. Town was out of sight and there were no lights. The Milky Way stretched beyond the trees in the lucid night, vast and remote. A creek ran down the hillside but they couldn't see it, there was only the sound of water moving in the dark. The air was heavy with the smell of rotting logs and the dank taste of moss and seeping melt.

Daniel glanced at the shadow of his brother.

"They just called you in there and offered it to you?"

"That's right," John said.

"What did Angeline say?"

"She's for it."

Daniel looked off in the dark.

"Well you deserve it if anyone does."

"Thanks."
"Be careful down there."
"You know it."

9

In the first slate-colored light the men came off the trucks and staggered down the slope toward the hole. In the woods along the edge of the camp the mist rose out of the scrub in the cold dawn air. The trees were still bare but the hills were not as stark. The hard bleak look had shifted into a hazy iron gray.

Among the men the brothers walked together in silence. John smoked and near the hole threw the stub down in the cinders along the tracks. Inside the mouth of the tunnel they stopped and lit their lamps. He knelt to gather his tools and when he looked up Daniel was watching him. When John had his gear loaded he stood and touched his brother's shoulder. A ways down the passage they turned away from each other and split up without saying anything, with just a look.

The engineer was already waiting for him at the end of the tunnel. He stood with a drafting board studying the tunnel roof and the heading of blank rock. Along the wall coal shone black and lustrous. The grate of metal wheels pulled over rails echoed down the passage, the dull knock of mule's hooves moving along the wooden ties. John came up and shook hands with the engineer.

He looked at the board and the sketched plan pinned down at the corners. A warren of tunnels penciled in dark heavy lead. The men leaned together and spoke in voices raised over the metallic whine of car trains and the rumble of distant blasts. The calls of miners came in broken echoes through the chambers. Voices decayed and died, incomprehensible in the noise. The engineer gestured toward the rock wall at the end of the passage.

"Beyond this shale lens we believe the seam pitches down sharply," he said. "It may only take a few blasts to get through. That's going to be your critical time."

John nodded. He looked at the engineer.

"I don't want to lose any men on this."

"All right then. Listen here. When you blast through this lens you're going to have a window of time where you can get men down in there with timbers, before the overburden starts to settle. There's a lot of mountain above you and it all wants to come down."

He studied John for a moment.

"Now we're not talking about a lot of time. You want to get as many props set as you can, as quick as you can. That's going to be your most dangerous time. There's your risk. How many men do you want to put down there?"

"That's the question."

The engineer shook his head. "Why in the hell they wanted it done like this I don't know."

"Well, they did."

"I know it," the man said. "All right then. Good luck. I'll be back down this evening to look at what you got done."

They shook hands and John thanked him and the engineer started back down the tunnel. John watched the man's lamp flash against the dark rock and then it was gone. He stepped through the doorway into the chamber and looked at the crew. They were crouched along the walls of the room talking in low voices. They turned and looked at him and waited.

"All right," he said. "Let's go. Get it mucked out. Let's get her ready to drill."

Five men came down with shovels and cleared the loose scree away from the heading, pitching it out along the sides of the tracks. The work kicked up a thick black dust that hung in the dank air. The muckers made sure the rails were clear and then retreated down the passage. When it was clear they brought up the big pneumatic drill on a carriage and pushed it flush against the face of the rock as far as the tracks ran.

John gave the signal and they started the machine. The drill operators wore steel masks and heavy leather aprons. A shielded lamp fixed on the carriage illuminated the wall of dark rock. The bit spun with a high-pitched whine and the deeper hiss of the pressurized air from the hose. The drill chewed into the soft rock and spat hot stone chips out over the machine and across the floor. They could smell the heating metal. When the bit started to smoke they stopped the drill and a man ran up and poured water over it. When it had cooled down they started again. They drilled two dozen holes in the rock face in horizontal rows and pulled the carriage back.

John called the next group of men and they came down to the wall and started sliding sticks of dynamite deep into the blast holes. Next they pushed in primer and finally they packed clay dummies behind the powder squibs with long steel tamping poles. When the men drew back he could see the pattern of holes over the face of the wall and the fuses hanging out of each hole. John cleared everyone back out of the tunnel and around the corner into the chamber. He called two men into the passage and sent them down to the wall. They lit candles and ghostly light bloomed against the rock. Carefully and quickly they began lighting the fuses.

John stood in the doorway of the side chamber and watched them. They were only shadows against the wall as the shifting beams of their cap lights lit the rock. The yellow candle flames moved back and forth in the dark as they quickly lit one fuse after another. The fuses hissed and the sharp odor of the smoke drifted up the tunnel. They lit the last fuse and he stood waiting for them in the doorway as they hurried back down the tunnel. Inside the chamber the men looked up as they entered. The whole crew was crouched along the far wall of the room under the strongest props. They all shut their eyes tightly and covered their ears.

There was a silence and a moment of stillness and then the shock of the blast and roaring and a concussion and a hail of splintered rock. The floor shook and the air rushed out and then back instantaneously. The bitter taste of burnt powder hung in the stale air. John went into the hall and looked. A cloud of rock dust hovered in the tunnel. He turned back into the room. The blast still rang in his ears.

"All right," he said. "One more time. Muckers come on. Let's go."

The men came out into the passage with shovels and turned their lamps on the heading. A vast gouge gaped in the shale but no coal shone in the shifting light. The men stopped and pulled filthy bandannas up over their mouths and noses and came down like robbers into the heaped debris. They pulled the first empty car down to the edge of the rubble and started loading the broken rock.

A driver led an ash-colored mule down the tracks toward them. He turned it by the bit and the animal stood passively as he chained the harness to the first car. The animal watched them, its big eye glistening in the lamplight. They lined up a train of empties on the track and when a car was full they tipped the empty cars off the track. Then the mule pulled the loaded car by and they brought up the next empty. They filled several cars and the mule pulled them off down the tracks. When they had mucked out the rubble they brought the drill carriage back down and started again.

When the drill had been pulled back and they were ready for the second blast, they withdrew again to the chamber and John sent two men down to light the fuses. Again the crew crouched along the wall of the chamber and waited. Again the boom and roar of the dynamite and shattering rock and the dying echo of the blast. For a moment John listened. There was the whisper of trickling water. He stood and looked into the tunnel and he could see the black sheen of the water seeping through the splinters of rock. He turned to the crew crouched along the wall.

"All right," he said. "We're through. There's water but it doesn't look too bad. Come on let's get this mucked out. Tell them to start bringing the timbers down."

The man called for the driver and John started down through the rubble toward the heading. At the end of the hall the blast hole gaped chest high in the rock. It was pitch black inside and he could not see down into it. Dark water still seeped out along the bottom. He turned his lamp down into the fissure and the coal glittered jet-black under the light. Down the tunnel a mule appeared pulling a train out of the dark. The cars were loaded with thick round beams glistening dull black with creosote. John called out to the men and his voice echoed down the passage.

"All right now—come on boys—get them timbers up—let's get set in here—"

The men started to move, wheezing in the close atmosphere. The air tasted stale and sulfurous. With the dust still hanging opaque in the tunnel and the dark water seeping in around their feet, they stabbed their shovels into the last of the black rubble. Other men started hauling the blackened timbers out of the cars and down toward the new hole gaping dead black in the wounded rock.

The men emerged from the dark of the tunnel mouth into the gray of falling dusk. Their voices came up echoing in the camp. Their cap lights were extinguished, their pale faces blackened with powder and soot. In the gloom the tips of their cigarettes glowed red as they lit them. The trucks were dark hulks parked along the ridge. The men crested the slope laughing, their filthy jackets draped triumphantly over their shoulders.

They leaned against the idling truck and smoked, grinning and joking laconically. The hanging exhaust an ashen plume in the dusk. Down the hill the last remnant of men straggled up through the camp. John climbed up in the bed and reclined in the corner and found a cigarette. Daniel stood grinning at the edge of the payload, leaning down and pulling tired men up into the bed and stowing their gear.

"You should've been down there with us," a man said.

"I know it," Daniel said.

"I tell you what son, you should've seen it. The way we blew that heading. It was something."

"Well all right then. Let's celebrate. Who's got the white lightning?"

"I figured you would," a man said.

"Get your ass up in here," Daniel said, grinning.

They were only shadows as they clowned around, silhouettes miming each other in the dusk. They laughed and acted out the events of the day. John glanced back down across the camp toward the company house. The blinds were drawn in the office, a light burning in the window behind them.

A man climbed in and crouched in the corner opposite John, grinning at him.

"We blew some rock today, didn't we?"

"Yes sir," John said. "We did."

John's cigarette dangled unlit at the side of his mouth. His eyes were smiling. The man reached over. His steel lighter shone dully in the twilight. John leaned down and lit his smoke and nodded mutely to him. Then he leaned back and inhaled deeply and closed his eyes. When everybody was loaded a man dropped his arm outside the truck bed and struck its steel flank. The driver glanced back and they gave him the sign. He let off the brake and shifted the truck in gear.

They came down the hollow in the twilight and turned onto the black asphalt along the mountainside. At the crossroads on the edge of town they filed down off the truck beds and scattered along the tracks. Some of the men started walking up the road toward the woods. John stopped and called after them.

"All right boys. Thanks. See you all tomorrow."

"See you in the morning," they said, turning back. "Good job today."

They waved and turned away and walked off along the tracks, silhouetted in the failing light with their empty dinner buckets. John and Daniel started down the street over the low hill into town. Along the last few houses they split off from the rest of the men.

"Night boys."

"All right then," they said.

At the end of the street Angeline stood on the porch and watched them come up the road. They looked up and saw her and she waved. Daniel raised his arm in reply. A dog ran out into the road, wagging its tail submissively. Behind them in the west the clouds towered in a vast rose-colored tapestry. The sun glinted red as it sank behind the dark line of the mountains. She raised her hand and shaded her eyes from the brilliant light. With her other hand she waved to them again and she was smiling.

At the moment before dawn the sky over the hollow was dark, streaked with reefs of low cloud that caught the first faint glow out of the east. The camp was still, the windows of the company house vacant and black. At the top of the hill one of the guards came out and stood in the road. He pulled his coat tight in the cold and stretched and blinked in the half-light. He lit a cigarette and looked back toward the guard shack. Through the doorway another man sat leaning over the stove. The sound of the truck engines came distant and faint somewhere down the hollow.

Before it was fully light the miners were already underground. The crew gathered their tools and lit their lamps and together started the half-mile down into the mountain to the seam. They walked mute along the passage, their boots shuffling in the dark. When they reached the chamber they scattered along the walls and stowed their gear.

John went into the passage. A man stood in the tunnel with a hose sprinkling down the rock dust. The water muddied the shale under his boots. He looked around for the fire boss but did not see him anywhere. John figured he must have already come and gone. He continued on to the heading. The men were starting to come down the hall behind him. He moved along the walls and checked the props. The new timbers gleamed black with creosote under the glare of his lamp.

Back in the tunnel the men were starting to gather in the chamber. John stepped down the steep pitch to inspect the new seam. The space was low and narrow, the coal glistening black under his light. He crouched against the wall and closed his eyes, inhaling. He frowned and smelled the air again. It was stale and didn't taste right. He opened his eyes and looked back. The men were coming down the tunnel toward him. He stood and yelled back down the hall, frantic.

"Boys, get back right now! Get out—"

There was a boom and a blinding white flash as the methane exploded and a roaring flame and the noise of shattering rock like dynamite and everything was blown back down the passage. The timbers cracked and splintered and the roof buckled and caved and everything went black in the collapse, burying everyone.

A blinding cloud of shattered rock and coal dust rolled down the shaft. Dust boiled everywhere in an impenetrable cloud. Every lamp was snuffed out by the blast. Someone was screaming that his leg was caught. At the edge of the wreck clouds of smoke drove miners back choking. In the chambers beyond the collapse men ran helter-skelter in the hanging dust. In the dark they started digging and clawing at the rubble, helpless and frantic.

Everything was black. John tried to move. His legs were pinned. He was caught in what felt like a pocket of darkness. He could hear their voices calling out, but he couldn't move or get enough breath to call back. He choked and struggled to pull himself out but he couldn't feel his legs and his back was numb. He could hear faint muffled cries somewhere under the rock.

A miner bellowed down the tunnel, his voice hoarse and ragged.

"Dig em out! Dig em out!"

Somewhere a voice wept faintly in the dark.

"Oh Jesus," it said. "Oh Jesus."

10

After two hours of digging they started pulling bodies out. When they uncovered a man whose lamp was still flickering they hurried to see if he was breathing but none ever were. They found men frozen in different attitudes of death, posed according to their final act. Some looked as if they were still struggling to get away, their bodies stretched out in arrested flight. Men were buried with their arms over their faces, covering their eyes and mouths from debris. Still others shielded the bodies of their brothers as if they could save another man by their own sacrifice. A few were curled up like infants, as though they might escape death through sleep.

Their faces were gray with the pallor of death and coal dust. Their mouths filled with black grime. When they found a man whose eyes had been caught open in his final moment, they had to scrape out the grit impacted in his blackened eyeballs to close them for the last time.

John was one of the last unearthed. When they brushed his face clean of the rubble and dust, he looked almost serene. His legs were pinned under a shelf of rock and they had to work with sledgehammers for forty minutes before they could pry him loose. When they were able to clear the hole up to the last strip of track, they brought draft mules down pulling trains of empties and they started stacking the bodies in the cars. They didn't stop to tell who was who, and by then it didn't matter.

After the requiem they showed him for the last time. The undertaker had done a good job on him. He wore a dark suit and his face was clean and smooth and white. His hair was combed back and shone dark in the candlelight. The shroud was drawn over his legs where they had been pinned but his hands were perfect and whole, resting pale at his sides.

They lit candles for him and a blend of incense and singed wax lingered in the shadowed atmosphere. When everyone had looked at him for the last time, the undertaker came over and closed the casket. He took out a screwdriver and drove the last few screws into the dark varnished wood of the lid. Then they covered it with the pall.

It was the last day of winter. Pallid light slanted in the afternoon sky as if the sun had never fully emerged. We all came out of the church and stood as they loaded the coffin onto the bed of a truck waiting there. The driver pulled away and drove slowly down the gravel road along the river to the graveyard. The rest of us started walking the quarter mile after the truck. No one spoke. All I could hear was the fading murmur of the truck motor and the scratch of our shoes moving in the gravel.

At the graveyard the wrought iron gate stood open. The driver waited by the truck bed while the pallbearers took the coffin down and brought it through the gate. We filed in behind them into the yard. Along the path we passed a dozen fresh graves and dozen more gaping ready.

They set the coffin down on a dark cloth spread out by the grave. On one side a mounded hill of new dirt waited to be shoveled back. The dark wet smell of earth hung in the air. There was no headstone yet, just a plain whitewashed cross driven in the ground for a marker. The pallbearers stepped away from the casket back into the half-ring of mourners that had formed around the grave. I stepped forward and turned and faced them all.

Angeline stood in the crowd surrounded by miners and their wives and a few other new widows. She wore a plain black dress and a black hat and veil. She looked pale and tired but remained stoic, composed. Her green eyes had grown big in her drawn face. Daniel stood beside her and she held his arm. His face was blank and pale and unshaven. His eyes were stunned and slightly vacant.

I opened the book and the wind fluttered the pages. I had to hold them down while I read.

> *Where wast thou when I laid the foundations of the earth? Declare if thou hast understanding. Who hast laid the measures thereof, if thou knowest? Or who hath stretched the line upon it? Whereupon are the foundations thereof fastened? Or who laid the cornerstone thereof; When the morning stars sang together, and all the sons of God shouted for joy?*

When the service was over the pallbearers came forward for the last time and lowered the coffin into the ground with ropes. I watched Angeline. The last color drain from her face, and my heart broke for her. A woman holding a few white lilies went over and gave them to Angeline. She took them and stepped to the edge of the grave. She looked down into the ground for a moment and then let the flowers fall into the grave. They scattered in the dirt on the dark wood of the box. Then she turned away and took Daniel's arm and steadied herself.

A man came over with a spade and held it out to Daniel. He looked at it for a moment as if it didn't register. Then he took it and stepped over to the mound of fill. He leaned and drove the blade into the dirt, deliberate and solemn, lifting a measure of earth. He let it fall into the grave over the lilies and the coffin and his silent, covered brother. He poured just that one scoop, and then stood and stared until they took the spade out of his hands and led him off. Then they started shoveling the rest of the earth into the grave.

A lot of old boys died down there at that time. It was just part of working underground. People came together and helped each other in the ways that they could. Things happened without explanation and gradually wore them down. That's how it went. You started out with the world ahead of you and then things just seemed to close in. You held on tight to any shred of glory that blew in the door.

PART II

11

A shovel pitched coal into the stove of a steam engine glowing red-hot. The workman stooped and wiped sweat from his face backhanded with the blackened sleeve of his jersey. A dark oval of perspiration stained his back, soaking his overalls. He went back to his work and the spade again bit into the chipped black mineral. Outside the smokestack belched clouds of soot as the great blackened steel machinery of the locomotive wheels ground forward, driving the train on.

A plain-looking man in a worn gray suit and hat was sitting by a window in the coach. A battered leather valise on the seat beside him. He unfolded a Charleston newspaper issued March 21. The headline read WORST DISASTER IN COUNTY HISTORY, followed by the sub headline *40 Die in Mine Blast.* He studied the article for a few minutes, then folded the paper on the seat beside him. He stood and walked down the aisle through the door into the smoking car, taking his worn valise with him.

The train rolled down the valley on tracks that followed the course of the wide brown river cutting through the mountains. The hills cradling the town were verdant with life and the first new growth of spring. The faint blush of redbud colored the mountains. Dogwoods on the verge of bloom and the earliest birds returning and building their nests.

The train slowed and stopped along the platform. He got up and took his bag, leaving the folded newspaper on the seat. He stepped down onto the platform and stood as the brakes unlocked and the engine lurched forward, gradually picking up momentum, leaving a cloud of lingering steam. He climbed down the depot stairs carrying his bag and started walking along the tracks toward town.

Certain hollows in that valley a stray spark had set off a mine fire. An old tunnel would catch light, the ancient dried out timbers burning out of control, igniting the black bituminous mineral. Whole tunnel cities of coal blazing underground, burning and no way to stop it. On and on, day and night. Consuming itself but never going out. Still burning to this day I expect.

Homer talked about the afterlife. A big dark cavern underground, souls flitting around everywhere, shadowy like bats with no memory or sense at all. Just ghosts lacking the power to remember anything—who they were, what they cared about. If they were fed a little blood though they could recall their lives, tell you about where they were from, what they thought about being dead, what they most desired from our world.

Only a few special people went to a place called Elysium when they died. There were deer, flowing rivers, fireflies in the fields, blackberries, and muscadine grapes. There were trout in the streams, partridge, wild honey, and apple trees—changing seasons—

◆ ◆ ◆

In the evening they sat together in the field at the edge of the garden. The light thickened in the sky. Streaks of day still glimmered in the west. It was warm for late March and the breeze moved over the grass, stirring the spring buds in the branches. Daniel watched the wind in the treetops across the river.

"I see things that I want to tell him about."

"I know," Angeline said. "I dream about him at night."

He stared off, remembering. "That son of a bitch was so damn good at everything."

He grinned and shook his head.

"One time when we were kids, we jumped the fence into the orchard out at Garvey's place. Night so clear you could see every star. He climbed all the way up the trellis onto the side of the house and was talking to Mary Garvey through her bedroom window. I could see their silhouettes up there. He told me to just keep picking up apples, but I was so scared I kept dropping them. I managed to get myself shot with rock salt for my trouble. Hole this size in my britches. He was already over the fence and gone."

He smiled for a moment, then his smile faded away.

"I never did know my mama and daddy," he said. "At least I don't remember if I did. I was too little. Daddy died in a rock fall. After that they said mama fell apart. They had to put her in the state hospital. She died in the asylum up in Boone county."

He turned and looked at her.

"Then they sent us down here and Peach looked after us. Taught us everything about the woods. Took us out to shoot squirrels. After he died, John was all I had. We were both working underground by the time I was twelve. He took care of me. All I ever had to do was watch him to learn anything I needed to know."

He paused and looked off at the water.

"I always had him to be smarter and stronger," he said softly.

She watched the river and the pattern of light shimmering on its surface. When she spoke her voice seemed distant, directed at no one.

"I just want to say the things I never said to him."

Daniel looked at her. Her eyes were shining in the twilight. He watched her for a moment, hesitating. Then under the deepening blue dusk he reached over and took her hand.

12

Two weeks passed before I saw David again. By then it was early April. I walked the two miles from the rectory along the river toward town. The evening was clear and crisp and fragrant with dogwood and apple blossom. A quarter moon fell into the pines. The woods between the train tracks and riverbank were alive with the drone of crickets and the deeper calls of frogs. Outside of town you could see every star but they would dim as you approached the lights of the houses. I stopped in the dusk and watched the shadow of a heron hunting the muddy bank.

I came up the road and turned and started across the field. The superintendent's house was up the hill a piece, commanding a view of the town and the valley. By the time I arrived it was fully night. The house was dark except the porch lamp and the glow of firelight in the parlor window. I went up on the porch and rang the bell. In a minute Sarah came to the door and let me in and took my coat and hat. I went down the hall and found David by the fire. The board was ready. He got up and we shook hands. He went over in the corner and put on a record and we stood by the fire and smoked cigars.

Later we sat by the hearth and studied the board at the low table with our customary tray of whiskey and ice. We played several games and I thought I had the upper hand a number of times only to be outfoxed in the end.

"You're enjoying quite a streak," I said.

He just grinned and kept studying the board and didn't say anything. After a minute he took a breath as if he wanted to say something but decided against it. I watched him.

"What is it?"

"How is John Black's widow getting along down there by herself?"

I stopped and looked up from the board. I sighed and reflected a moment.

"Well, she's a strong woman," I said. "But it's not going to be easy for her. She has a few people around to lean on. Otherwise I'd be worried."

I focused back on the pieces. When I looked up at him again he was watching the fire.

It had already begun to turn warm and the air smelled of fresh vegetation washed clean by rain. The grass was still damp from the morning dew and the heat of the afternoon sun mixed with gusts of cool breeze and the fleeting shadows of clouds in the electric metamorphosis of spring.

Angeline worked in the garden behind the house. The ground was turned in the straight dark serried rows. She knelt in the loam and spread compost and seeded early corn out of her apron pocket. She wore a faded blue dress and a man's worn brown leather shoes and an apron stained with coffee grounds, hearth ash, and sawdust. A black ribbon held her hair back out of her face and she was flushed with color and sweat and grime. She watched a blue jay dart out of the branches to the ground gathering fibers for its nest.

There was the sound of a car out in the road. She looked up the slope and watched a black Ford slow down and stop in front of the house. After a minute a man got out and came through the gate and disappeared onto the porch. She turned back to planting.

David held the screen door open and knocked. He waited. He knocked again. After a few moments he let the door close and came down off the porch and started walking through the yard around the side of the house. He turned the corner and saw her kneeling in the garden.

"Hello?"

She turned her head and saw him at the side of the house. He came on toward her and she watched him. She wiped her face on her dress sleeve. He stopped at the edge of the garden.

"Afternoon, mam."

"Afternoon."

"My name is David—"

"I know who you are."

Her voice was not unkind but spoken as if she were waiting for him to say what he had come for.

"I just wanted to come down here and see how you were getting along."

She resumed digging. She was so natural and graceful in her movement that there was nothing rude or peremptory in it.

"Have you been able to get by on what the company settled you with?"

She kept working. She didn't look at him.

"I'm alive," she said.

There was silence except the scratch of the trowel in the soil.

"Well, I wanted to invite you up to the house for Easter dinner. I know it's a few weeks off yet, but I hope you might consider coming. I'm having Father Nate and some folks over after church and I would be pleased if you could be with us."

"Father Nate?"

"Yes mam. We're buddies you could say. He lets me beat him at chess sometimes."

She dug in her apron for corn and dropped a few kernels in the earth.

"Well, I don't know," she said after a moment. "My sister is having people in Montgomery."

He moved slightly as if to speak but didn't say anything.

"I don't think I'll be able to," she said, finally glancing at him. "I thank you for your invitation, though."

"Well, you're welcome in any case, if it suits you. We would all be pleased to have you. Let me know if there's anything I can do. Or let Father Nathan know—"

He trailed off, unsure. She went back to weeding. He watched her, hesitating for a moment. Then he pushed his hair back and put on his hat.

"Mam," he said.

He turned and started back around the house to the car. She looked up for a moment and watched him go.

13

I left the car on the side of the road and started up through the yard. I went up on the porch and listened. The front door stood open. I knocked on the screen door and looked back into the shadowed house. Mary Beth came out of the back room. She smiled weakly when she saw me. She opened the screen and stood in the doorway.

"This isn't necessary, Father," she said. "Ed's working again. We're all right now."

I shook my head and put on a mock-serious tone.

"There's nothing I can do about it," I said. "It's not up to me. I have strict instructions to deliver this."

I held out the envelope. "This is the last time, I promise. You'll be doing me a favor if you take it."

She stared at it, hesitating. Finally she saw that I wasn't going to let her refuse, and she took it and seemed relieved. She looked out across the field toward David's place.

"Tell the superintendent thank you for us," she said without looking at me.

I didn't say anything for a moment. Then I nodded.

"All right," I said.

Daniel's shack sat way up the hollow in the woods on land the company owned but nobody looked after. He had built it there himself with his brother's help several years earlier. It was just one room with a stove in the middle and a steel pipe up through the roof for a chimney. A battered desk and chair against the far wall. An iron cot in the corner under the window with an old leather trunk at its foot. There was no plumbing, just a chamber pot, and he drew his water from the creek. In the winter he had to break the crust of ice on the surface and dip the pail down underneath to fill it.

There was no road up there, just a path, and every morning he walked down the hollow three miles and followed the tracks to the crossroads where the trucks took them to the camp. Nobody else lived out there and there was no gas or power line. He had no radio and after dark he would sit up in bed by the lantern and chew tobacco and pluck at an old mandolin missing several strings. He could hardly play but he had a good clear voice that could hold key and he liked to pick out bluegrass tunes.

He ate mainly out of cans except for what he shot himself. Squirrel, rabbit, dove, and an occasional woodchuck. He poached deer in every season and on Saturdays he was down at the river by dawn fishing along the muddy bank. His brother used to come out every few weeks to help him work on the place or split logs. They'd been planning to put up a woodshed or a smokehouse—they hadn't decided which. The last thing they'd done was raise a real outhouse with a door and a seat and everything.

In the cool of the morning he walked out in the woods with a stripped and broken tree branch as a walking stick. The April woods were alive with growth and rebirth. Light fell in broken shafts, dappling the path. From somewhere high up came the hollow knock of a woodpecker. Through the trees he could hear the murmur of the creek where rapids drove the water through the rocks.

In the undergrowth along the path there was a rustling. He stopped and listened. He stooped and with his stick cleared a layer of dead leaves and probed below. There beneath the leaves on the bare ground were two snakes mating, coiled up together roiling and seething in the earth.

In the afternoon Daniel walked along the railroad tracks beyond the edge of town. It already seemed late in the day. The sky had turned to lead, the light pale and diffuse. Loose spikes were scattered along the tracks, blackened with coal dust, the rails themselves stained dull black with graphite. The air was tinged with the chemical tang of rail ties steeped in creosote.

He kicked gravel along the track bed and threw away the stick he'd carried with him down out of the woods. He walked with his back to the light, his shadow slanting ahead of him in the weeds. Along the tree line above the road he glimpsed a ragged delta of geese turning north. They disappeared behind the hill and their honking calls faded gradually away and finally died.

He came down off the ridge of the tracks into a swale and cut across toward the woods. He passed into the trees, moving silently over the carpet of pine needles. He could taste the flavor of the evergreens. The shadow of the boughs was cool and he buttoned his jacket coming through the brush and put his hands in his pockets. He could smell the river and feel its raw damp breath. He crossed through the screen of trees into the ditch at the side of the road. He climbed up and looked back along the dirt track. Its dull ruddy surface curved toward town, disappearing in the trees. He turned the other way and walked on along the path by the roadside.

When he came around the bend the sun had started to descend, reddening a reef of cloud behind the hills. The churchyard was empty. The face of the building shone white in the clearing. The squat stone cross was the color of charcoal, its shadow leaning back against the church. He glanced across the field at the small rectory built back against the trees. No sign of anyone. He walked past the buildings, silent except the scrape of his boots in the rocks.

The black wrought iron gate was shut. Instead of checking to see whether it would budge he set his grip and made a deft low vault over the rail. He stopped and pulled his jacket down and looked back along the road. Then he turned and followed the path.

The new graves had settled by now and sagged faintly in the moist soil. The provisional whitewashed cross had been replaced by an austere slab of charcoal-colored granite. He sat on the ground in the stunted grass by the grave and looked across the field, out past the fence and the screen of trees to the river and the mountains beyond.

It was night by the time he got home. He came in the darkened room of the shanty and lit the lamp and got a fire going in the black iron stove. The room was disheveled and plain with little decoration or civilized touch of any kind. His mine clothes and cap lay draped over the back of a chair. A shotgun leaned in the corner. After a while coal burned in the stove with a bluish flame.

Thunder rolled somewhere far off. A moment later it started to rain, first in light patches then hard and continuous. The drops beat a hollow erratic tattoo on the tin roof. He leaned over in his chair and with an old tarnished fork stirred a can of beans heating on the top of the stove.

Late April brought sudden rains down the valley, driving the animals out of sight and leaving the dark boughs slick and burdened with water. The dogwoods offered white petals that spread and drooped under the weight of the raindrops. Farther back in the shadowed undergrowth, beyond the curtain of blossoms pied green and white, you could trace their inky trunks. Down the hill the river turned an uncertain shade of dark, discolored by the sudden runoff.

On those afternoons I sat up in bed by the window reading under the lamp. Through the window the sky was a dense continuous plane of gray, casting the valley in a lingering twilight. I lay there listening to the rain, and the thunder coming over the mountains in distant somber peals.

14

When she opened her eyes it was dark. John had been in the ground a month, but she still woke an hour before dawn and dressed and went in the kitchen to make breakfast. She sat up in bed and stretched. The air was cold. The empty glass ashtray sat by the lamp on the bedside table. Lying beside it was a black ribbon.

She got out of bed and took the ribbon and found the brush on the mantel. In the dark she ran the brush through her hair and pulled it back and tied it. She took off her nightgown and laid it over the back of the chair and pulled on a slip. She picked a dress out of the wardrobe and stepped into it and straightened her slip. She slid her feet into the worn men's brogans by the bed and went out.

The kitchen was cold. She turned on the lamp and lit the gas. On the counter she set out buttermilk, eggs, butter, lard, and flour. She mixed biscuit dough from scratch and floured the board and rolled and cut them and laid them out in the pan. The oven was warm and ready and she put the biscuits in and the coffee on to boil. The sky gradually lightened in the windows. Finally the sun glinted over the edge of the hills.

When the biscuits were ready she emptied them into a basket lined with a cloth napkin. They steamed in the early morning cold. She sat and drank coffee and ate only one biscuit with butter and honey. She left the rest sitting wrapped in a cloth napkin in the basket.

When she finished eating she put the plate in the sink and took off her apron and folded it over the chair. She went into the bedroom and took off her shoes and unbuttoned her dress and stepped out of it and stood in her slip. She folded the dress over the back of the chair on top of the nightgown. She went into the washroom and pulled off her slip and stood naked. She leaned over the basin and scrubbed her face and washed under her arms and between her legs. She rinsed and dried herself and put on the robe and came back into the bedroom.

Outside it was fully morning now, the pale light filtering through the curtains into the stillness of the room. She opened the wardrobe and took down a plain black dress on a hanger. On the chest of drawers in the corner there was a small cherry wood box. She opened it and took out the dark string of a rosary, letting her fingers run over the smooth hard surfaces of the beads.

She sat down on the side of the bed still holding the rosary in one hand. She covered her eyes with the other hand and her face fell apart and the tears started rolling down. Her breath caught in long muted spasms as she cried.

The bell rang and families came down the hard dirt path past the stone cross in the yard. They stood out in the grass and shook hands and embraced. The stunned children waited in the field, their faces scrubbed pale in the cold morning light. A few girls had on starched bonnets and white gloves and dresses embroidered with pastel flowers, but most slouched in hand-me-down outfits carefully ironed and kept hanging all year in closets to look fresh.

In the field the tulips and apple trees were in full bloom. Beyond the graveyard and across the valley the lower slopes of the mountains were already green. Only the peaks remained gray. Half a moon drooped pale in the daylight. The air smelled of dogwood blossoms, dewy grass, and the strong raw presence of the river.

The miners and their wives and were all in their best clothes, the one dark suit kept for Easter and weddings and funerals. Some of the widows were still in black and came in sullen and hushed with their children huddled around them. They settled along the pews with the bell yet ringing and sat in the cool dark hall staring at the dusty prayer books in the racks. Other families still mixed in the yard. Finally the bell knolled its last and the others filed in the doors and settled along the pews as the organ started in the loft. I could hear the muted scuff of boot heels on the worn floorboards.

Two candles burned on the altar. The acolytes lit the incense and the last candles with their poles and came and stood behind the rail while the organ generated its hoarse music. They brought the vessels out of the sacristy and laid them out along the credence.

I stepped out of the vestry into the apse and touched the water in the basin. I crossed myself. The organ stopped and you could hear the machine creak in the loft, and the deep hushed breath of the flock and the sharp hack of a cough somewhere in the back. I began the Mass.

In nomine Patris—

I looked out along the benches. I thought I saw David sitting alone in the far corner, shadowed along the outer aisle. I opened the book, turning the gilded edges of its pages, and found the place.

> *And behold, there was a great earthquake: for the angel of the* LORD *descended from heaven, and came and rolled back the stone from the door, and sat upon it. His countenance was like lightning, and his raiment white as snow: and for fear of him the keepers did shake, and became as dead men.*

I kept scanning the pews but saw neither Angeline nor Daniel there. After the prayer for the dead I made the Lord's prayer. Then I gave the sign. One by one, people went to the credence and opened the gate, taking their places along the aisle in front of the altar. I stepped down from the dais and called them all forward for the body and the blood.

In the afternoon children ran in the grass and chased each other along the edge of the woods. By then their collars were open and their neckties put away or flying loose. From across the field in their suits and dresses they looked like grown men and women gone mad in pursuit or flight. Their voices were clear and high like birdsong or chiming bells. I could hear them singing ring around the rosy pocket full of posy ashes ashes, until it came to a crescendo and ended in a shout and then started to build again. I stood out at the edge of the party and listened to them play. A little boy fell down hard in the grass and started to cry.

Sarah came out of the house with a tray of sandwiches and set it on the picnic table with the potato salad and slaw. Their mothers called the children in from the woods and took them all inside for lemonade while the men hid pastel tinted eggs in the grass. When they came out they had their baskets and were told that they just missed the Easter bunny and there he goes into the woods, you might see him if you run—

The children hunted eggs in the yard and we all watched the eager concentration in their faces as they scanned the turf for any glint of color. When they had found the last egg they all came around grinning and showing us their baskets. They lined up for more lemonade, spilling half of it in the ground before they could bring the cups to their mouths.

David knelt and spoke to a little girl, asking her about the dyed eggs she had found. She was very proud of them and was careful to point out to him where they had been in the yard and how she had found them and what color each one was. He moved among the guests talking with everyone and making them feel welcome, but he seemed preoccupied. I saw him glance at his pocket watch a few times.

By dusk only a few guests remained. The few children left were crying. Sarah was clearing away the dishes from the picnic tables. People stood in the corners of the field, their silhouettes leaning together in conversation, the tips of cigarettes glowing in the twilight. The last guests were gradually saying good night. David thanked each of them as they departed and shook their hands.

There was only a small group left. Won't you all come in for a drink, he said, and a few said why not and we all went in the house. We stood in the parlor around the fireplace. David poured brandy and came around with a cedar humidor offering the men cigars. He went in the corner and put jazz on the victrola. Everyone was talking and feeling good.

He walked back into the kitchen to say something to Sarah. When he came back to the front hall, Angeline was standing in the doorway. She wore an ivory-colored dress with a lace collar. Her dark hair fell on her shoulders. Her beauty was such that it struck him dumb. He stood in the hall and looked at her. She waited there uncertainly. After a moment he recovered and smiled and welcomed her in. He took her hand and looked into her eyes.

"I didn't think you were going to come."

She smiled sadly.

"I'm here," she said.

15

That night the town was cold and still. A few days yet before the year's last frost. Only the shadows of a few feral dogs moved in the road.

A light burned in the window of a small house near the river. Inside four men sat around the kitchen table smoking in the silence. Cigarette fumes hung in a blur under an electric bulb. Packs of camels and luckys littered the table among tarnished steel lighters. Their fingertips were stained with nicotine, coal dust, and the sharp gasoline odor of lighter fluid. A man chewed tobacco and every so often spit brown liquid into an empty coke bottle.

There was coffee brewing on the stove. A woman set dirty dishes in the sink to be washed. A radio turned way down played hillbilly music in some other room. The clink of dishes in the sink and the dull boil of the coffee percolating. A dog barked somewhere off in the dark.

She wiped her hands on her apron and took cups down out of the cupboard and set them on the table with a sugar bowl. She looked at the men.

"There's blackberry pie," she said.

Nobody answered. One of them looked up at her and shook his head no. She turned and took the pot off the stove and poured coffee into the cups. They nodded at her in thanks.

There was a knock on the screen door. The woman looked out through the window over the sink onto the darkened back porch but could discern nothing. She looked around the table at the men, hesitating a moment. They watched her as she frowned and turned to the door. She pulled it open. There were two men standing on the porch in the dark. She stepped back into the kitchen and they moved forward into the light.

One of the men was dressed in overalls and a flannel shirt and a wool hunting jacket. It was Ed Summers. The other one was shorter with a blank nondescript face and spectacles. He was small and unassuming, wearing a modest plain gray suit and hat and carrying a battered leather valise as if he were a businessman or salesman. Ed Summers nodded around the table in acknowledgement.

"Boys, this is Mr. Wilkinson," he said.

The plain-looking man stepped forward into the room. The men got up out of their chairs and looked at him. They stepped over from the table and one by one shook his hand. The woman went into the other room and came back with another chair and set it at the table. Mr. Wilkinson took off his hat and overcoat and handed them to her and she went into the other room. The men moved back to their places and sat. Mr. Wilkinson put his bag down on the floor at the foot of the chair and sat down at the table.

Beyond town there were no lights along the river. I went out in the evening after vespers when everyone had gone home and the church was empty and I walked along the banks. There was a trail down through the trees to the water. At night, looking back from the head of the path, the church and the rectory stood dark and silent, blue shadows at the edge of the woods.

I walked down through the trees, listening to the river. I would sit and pick out the constellations as I waited for moonrise. A fish odor hung in the dark, with the blunt wet smell of mud and sand. Even in winter when everything looked dead and a crust of ice had formed along the edge, I would find a place on the sloping bank and sit until the cold was too much.

Now in early spring the valley was still raw and bleak, but I could feel the surge of an invisible force. In the late afternoon the sunlight reflected on the surface of the water, breaking into brilliant shimmering scales. At dusk the light was a diffuse and sourceless glow. The water was calm and would change color from brown to green and finally a clear iridescent blue and gold. Then it was like a mirror, and in it every tree along the river, and above them the mountains and clouds, had their own golden twin, an inverted world underwater that was still and perfect and eternal. I loved to be there and watch that shift. And when the vision faded in the nightfall and the river darkened into a deep opaque slate gray, I lingered there ruminating, illuminated in its afterglow.

In the dark I left the river and climbed back up the hill toward the rectory. It was a small modest house across the empty yard from the church. I came in the door and took off my muddy shoes and left them on the mat. It was cold in the hall. I hung up my coat and went in the kitchen and turned on the gas.

I went in the bedroom and turned on the light. It was clean and sparsely decorated with a crucifix above the bed and a picture of the Holy Virgin on the far wall. A washstand with a mirror and a basin stood against the wall by the door. On the bedside table a lamp and a pitcher of water with a glass. By the lamp a stack of books and letters and my reading glasses. I took the letters and eyeglasses and went into the kitchen.

There was roast beef in the icebox, pink and rare and sliced thin. I made a sandwich with horseradish and sat at the kitchen table and ate it with leftover potato salad. I opened the letters and read them while I ate. After a while I went into the bedroom and got a pen and stationery out of the desk and went back into the kitchen and wrote a few responses.

When I had eaten I changed into nightclothes and washed my face. I went in the kitchen and turned the gas down and got into bed. I sat up against the headboard and put on my reading glasses and took one of the books from the table.

I opened it to the bookmark. The left page was Greek text, its alphabet florid with accents and breathing marks. The right page was filled by a color plate of the rape of Persephone. Her ravisher emerged from the underworld into an open meadow driving a gilded, midnight-colored chariot drawn by two coal black immortal horses. She was startled, spilling a basket of spring flowers that she had gathered, the blossoms falling in a brilliant carpet that covered over the earth.

16

The moon was a waning sliver over the hills, and in the west the last trace of day faded from the horizon into the deeper blue of the night sky, luminous and immaculate. Daniel came around the side of the house and looked down toward the kitchen window. There was a lamp burning there and he saw a shadow move across the light.

He walked up and stood by the window and looked between the curtains. Angeline was standing at the counter with her back turned. He tapped on the windowpane. She turned around and looked but saw only her own reflection in the dark glass. She came over to the window and peered out. She saw him standing out in the dark. She smiled and signaled him to come around to the back of the house.

He grinned and nodded and went on back through the yard. He climbed up on the porch in the dark. She came out the screen door and embraced him and kissed him. From her body he smelled soap and earth and the salt perfume of clean sweat.

"Sit down," she said. "I have a surprise."

She went back inside and he sat on a cane-backed chair and waited. A moment later she came out with a mason jar. She held it up in the light shining through the kitchen window. A thick amber liquid glowed inside. Submerged in the bottom of the jar was a solid shard like a shadow in the gold.

She twisted the lid off the jar and held it out to him smiling. He looked at her and then reached bearlike with his fingers down into the jar and pulled up the chunk of honeycomb. He held it over his mouth and let it drip onto his tongue and down his throat. It was lovely and viscous and sweet and had a deep wild tang. He let it all drizzle into his mouth and then sucked and chewed at the wax.

She watched him and smiled. They sat there on the dark porch with the open jar and ate honey in the dark. They sat for a while, silent and content. He licked the drops off his fingers and she went inside and brought back a damp rag and they wiped their hands and mouths clean.

She studied him in the lamplight. He was fully groomed and shaved. She noticed the gleam of brilliantine combed into his hair.

"You look nice," she said.

"I'm tired of living out there with the animals."

"You can't stay up that hollow forever."

"No, I guess not," he said. "For a long time I thought I could."

He looked at her. "It's you I'm worried about," he said. "There's no way you can make it on what they settled you with."

Her eyes fell away. She looked off into the dark. "I'm doing all right," she said softly.

"A woman can't make it down here alone," he said. "Not these days. You know that."

He turned his body and faced her. She didn't look at him.

"I have some money saved," he said. "I want to take care of you. We can take care of each other."

She looked at him and her face softened. She took his hand and held it between her warm hands.

"You know I love you, Daniel," she said. "I always will."

She leaned over and kissed him on the temple.

"You'll always be my brother."

Late Saturday afternoon I was out in the yard in shirtsleeves driving nails into a few loose fence pickets. It was warm and the sky was a clear brilliant blue. I heard a sound and looked up and saw a black car coming down the road. I stood up holding the hammer and a handful of nails and watched David pull up. Dust hung in the road behind the Ford.

He got out and waved and came over to the fence. I poured the nails into my pocket and we shook hands. I was facing the afternoon sun and I shaded my eyes with my hand.

"I don't see you down here much outside the occasional Sunday," I said. "You should come down more often."

"I just stopped by to see if you'd care to come up to the house for supper tonight. If you want, I can wait and we'll go back in the car."

"Why don't we give poor Sarah a break from cooking? Come on inside and I'll fix us something. Somebody just gave me a pint of apricot brandy. We can try her out."

"All right."

We went in the house. It was cool and dark inside. I put the hammer down and took the nails out of my pocket and put them on the end table. I went in the kitchen and came back with an unmarked pint bottle of clear syrupy liquid and two glasses. We sat in the cool shade of the front room. The afternoon the sun flooded in, orange and gold over the edge of the hills. The shadows of the pines lengthened in the field. It was quiet and cool and serene. The sunlight flashed in our eyes. I poured two shots of the liquor and we made a wordless toast and drank. It was sugary and burned going down, and left the essence of apricots in your mouth.

"This stuff is tasty," he said.

"Not bad."

"Kind of sweet though."

I poured two more shots and we drank those more slowly.

"What's on your mind? I know you didn't come down here just for my cooking."

"I came to talk to you."

"Talk."

"I wanted to ask you about Angeline Black," he said. "Your opinion."

I glanced at him, fingering my glass.

"She's a special woman," I said. "That's clear. And she's up there on her own without much help. But for God's sake, her husband's been dead less than six weeks. She doesn't know up from down right now. Give her some time to grieve properly and bury him in her heart."

He nodded a moment and looked out along the trees.

"I intend to start courting her," he said.

"People in this town might not be so understanding. They're going to talk."

"Let them talk. I've been alone a long time. Am I asking for too much to have a woman and be happy?"

He looked at me. I didn't say anything.

"My God, I've never felt this way in my whole life," he said. "She's all I can think about, Nathan. When my wife died, down inside myself it was like I died with her. I couldn't feel anything. I was numb and I lived like that for years. I thought I'd go on that way forever."

He watched me. "Now this woman makes me feel something," he said. "Not giddy on the surface but deep down. Like I'm connected to the rest of the world. Like there's always been a union behind things and now I'm finally aware of it and I can be a part of it."

"Sounds like you got it bad."

He shook his head vaguely and looked away. "I believe she cares for me too," he said.

For a moment I watched him. He was looking off in the distance. The sky was turning red and gold over the mountain, a deep violet behind the trees.

"That may be so," I said finally. "But it doesn't mean she's ready for anything but healing herself. Getting back on her feet. Look, all I'm saying is try and take it easy with her for a while. Just don't do anything drastic."

17

David got up from his desk and stretched and looked out the window. The sky was perfect. Bright sunlight washed down the hollow and a breeze moved the leafy flanks of the hills. The men yet underground, the camp as still in the spring afternoon as if it had been abandoned. He closed the blinds and turned away from the window and went back to the desk. He put a few papers into a manila folder and tied a string around it and put it in his bag. He turned off the lamp and came around the desk and took his coat and hat down from the rack. He came out and locked his office and stood at the door holding his hat and overcoat.

The secretary looked up from her typewriter.

"I'm going to go on a little early," he said. "See you in the morning."

"All right."

There were a few cars in the office lot. He got in the black Ford and turned the engine and backed out. He stopped and shifted gears and looked down toward the mine. The hole gaped there dark and bottomless. He turned the wheel and pulled away. The guards waved from the door of the booth as he drove up and out of the camp.

The car came down the gravel road into the valley and turned onto the blacktop toward town. He passed the filling station on the hill and slowed down at the bottom, turning across the tracks onto the main street toward the river. Boys were out along the tracks leaving pennies on the rails to be smashed under the next train.

The road turned into a dirt track at the top of the low hill. He slowed the car and drove down the alley past the last houses. He parked and went through the open gate toward the house. He didn't go to the front door but walked straight around the side.

Small blue flowers had already begun to open in the side beds along the edge of the yard. Dandelions sprouted in the grass under the fence. When he came around to the back he stood and looked at the dark ridges of earth turned in precise rows running down the mild grade of the field.

Angeline was at the bottom of the hill beyond the garden. Under the apple tree stood three white hives along the wire fence. She was working at one of the wooden boxes. The dark specks of a few disturbed bees swirled in loose orbits around her. She looked up toward the house and saw him there. She waved and started coming up the slope.

He looked up at the tree shadowing the house. There was a crow moving in the branches. The feathers under its wings shone a lustrous black, almost blue in the sunlight. It bobbed and flapped as a pair of blue jays lunged around it trying to drive it away. The crow took off over the roof and disappeared and the jays lit out after it.

Her hair was tied back and she had on her stained apron and men's brogans. She carried a pail of clippings and weed roots for compost. She was smiling and flushed with color.

Her skin had the golden cast of the year's first sun. He took off his hat and watched her come.

"Afternoon."

"Afternoon," she said, coming up through the grass along the garden's edge.

"I hope you don't mind me calling like this."

She looked at him and a faint smile crossed her lips.

"Could I have stopped you?"

He grinned. "I guess not."

She set the pail down in the grass and faced him with her hand shading her eyes from the sun.

"How are your bees?"

"They're alive," she said. "I think they made it through the winter all right."

He gestured at the garden with his hat. "It looks like you've been busy."

"Today is the new moon," she said. "I have a few days to put my beans in and whatever flowers I want. Another week for gourds and melons. Yesterday was my last day for potatoes. Anything that grows underground goes in with the waning moon. Tubers and root vegetables. The rest between the new and full moon."

She turned toward a small plot along the fence near the house.

"Here are my herbs," she said. "By summer I'll have rosemary, fennel, and rue. And along here violets and dark blue pansies are already coming up. Columbines here. I love their red flower. And daisies along here soon."

She shaded her eyes again and looked at him. "Can I offer you something to drink?"

"All right."

She walked up the steps through the screen door and went inside and came back with two glasses of iced tea. They sat on the back steps in the shadow of the house looking down toward the river. He took a drink. The tea was sweet and cool and faintly bitter. They sat and drank the tea and watched the clouds move behind the mountains on the other side of the river. On a branch above the house a squirrel hung upside down gnawing frantically at the green unopened buds, its tail jerking for balance.

He watched her gazing out along the valley. She studied every tone of green from the deep shadows along the river to the mottled tops of the hills.

"It was real nice to have you up at the house last week," he said.

He stopped and she gave a slight nod in the silence. He watched her until she looked him in the eyes.

"I want to see you again," he said.

She nodded and looked away.

"I know," she said softly.

I saw them often in those weeks. In the evenings after supper he would go down into town and find her in the garden or working in the house. She would take off her apron and go with him and they would walk by the river until dark. Sometimes they came all the way out to the rectory and the three of us would sit and have a brandy and talk for a while.

One evening in late April I was sitting up reading and there was a knock. I went to the door and they were standing together on the steps. David smiled and smiled. They wanted me to come out with them. It was a warm clear night and the treetops were swaying in the breeze. We went out and sat in the field and watched the moon rise and the stars appear in the dimming sky. They sat near each other but I never saw their hands touch, even after the dusk had turned them into two shadows moving against the darker woods.

The next evening I was invited up to the house. When I got there they had already eaten supper and were in the parlor with a fire going. Angeline sat on the hearth, quiet and serene, her eyes shining in the firelight. The three of us had a bourbon and listened to the radio for a while. Then David got up feeling hilarious with whiskey and shut the radio off and looked at me. He gestured at the piano.

"Why don't you play a bit for us there, Father?"

I drained my drink and grinned at him. "Only if you will ask Sarah to come in and sing."

"My pleasure."

He went in the hall and called to Sarah in the kitchen to come join us. She came in smiling and taking off her apron. He fixed her a whiskey and insisted she drink it immediately. I sat down at the piano and Sarah sat by me on the bench holding her drink. Angeline sat on the hearth and watched us. Her smile lit up the room. David stood grinning in the middle of the rug conducting us with a drink in his hand. Sarah had a lovely alto voice and could sing harmony. I asked her what songs she knew and started to work out the chords. Angeline just sat by the fire with her drink, listening, smiling her sweet sad way and letting her eyes close to the music.

I got to know Angeline better and I fell in love with her the way everyone did. She always was quiet around me, but when I looked into her liquid green eyes I sensed a keen mind and a curiosity for everything she saw and underneath it something else. A sort of mute compassion for the sad and wounded people and things she saw around her. At the same time she took childlike pleasure in her garden and in the beauty of the burgeoning world on the mountains along that valley.

18

The dusk deepened around them as they came down through the trees toward the water. The light barely lingered behind the shadow of the mountains in a region of shifting green, gold, and rose that faded into the deep blue of the encompassing night. The moon was a pale crescent like a tusk hung above the river, trembling at its zenith and starting to fall. Its ivory light shone in a swath over the face of the dark water like a fleeting, ambiguous path. Stars winked on hesitantly and the whole valley was still, exhausted from its process of self-resurrection.

All around in the dark along the bank the voices of invisible insects and river frogs blended in a lush drone. The pair stepped out beyond the last trees and negotiated the steep wall of the bank. David reached back and took her hand as she came down onto the silty edge. He stood in shirtsleeves and she took off her shoes and felt the cool of the sand and the cobbles smoothed by water. A breeze came down out of the woods on the other side, alive with the taste of pine and musk and the sweet clean smell of new growth.

There was a cluster of white blossoms on a branch hanging over the water. She stepped into the shallows and reached up to pluck it. The dying light shone through the light cotton of her dress and the shadow of her body showed, backlit in the dusk. Her hair caught the glow like dark gold. She put the blossom behind her ear. She smiled. For the first time there was no sadness in her face. He kissed her hand. Then he pulled her to him and kissed her lips. She pulled gently away. He still held her hand. His voice was calm and solemn when he spoke.

"I want you to be my wife," he said.

Angeline looked at him and tried to smile, but a trace of pain was there. She looked away into the darker woods. Her voice seemed to come from a long way off.

"I'm not in love with you," she said.

He watched her for a long moment, the line of her profile in the dusk. Finally she looked back at him.

"That doesn't matter to me," he said.

Daniel came up the tunnel among the men. He tasted fresh air for the first time since before dawn. The burnt flavor of powder still lingered in his mouth, the stale breath of men and animals. His head throbbed with the remnant of some choking damp.

The atmosphere above ground was still warm from the afternoon heat. The men extinguished their lamps and started to peel off layers of filthy clothing. It was still full daylight, the sun hanging in the west for another hour. Low in the sky along the tree line the full moon rose like a pale, faded scar.

Daniel walked by himself to the last truck. He climbed up and sat in the corner by the tire well, waiting for the bed to fill with worn-out miners. He closed his eyes and he could hear the call and response of birdsong, and under it the clipped rhythm of the miners' laconic speech and the crunch of their boots in gravel.

He opened his eyes as another miner clambered up into the truck bed and settled in the corner across from him. The man grinned over at him with blackened teeth.

"What say there, Daniel."

"Henry."

Henry dug a glass bottle of clear liquid out of his overalls and uncapped it and took a swig. He closed his eyes as it went down and sighed with satisfaction. He looked at Daniel and offered the bottle without a word. Daniel accepted it and turned it up, taking a good long draw on the moonshine. The fumes burned the back of his throat and it went down with a shiver. He handed the bottle back to the man and nodded in thanks. Henry showed his ruined teeth again and gestured with the flask.

"There you go," he said. "What does a man good."

Henry took off his cap and combed down his filthy hair with his hand. He peered at Daniel and the whites of his eyes stood out against his blackened face.

"What do you have to say for your sister-in-law?"

"About what?"

"About how she's set to marry the superintendent."

Daniel looked at him.

"What the hell are you talking about?"

Henry's eyes fell away.

"I figured you would've already heard about it," he said.

Daniel shook his head and stared off in the woods. He didn't say anything else. He reached out his hand and Henry again passed him the flask. Daniel took another deep pull. The truck lurched off the brake and fell in gear and they took off down the road.

19

The full moon shone over the black line of the mountains, casting the sky around it a deep violet. Its beams diffused in the trees and lit the woods with a dim milky glow. Its gravity pulled at the world and every animal was alert, sniffing the potent spring air, its blood restless and alive. It shone so hard it dulled the stars, providing a ghostly twilight that was neither day nor night but something more rare and volatile.

The hollow was silent and the shack stood there derelict like an abandoned hideout or the rude lair of some eremite. Still and dark like a blue shadow against woods, the moonlight shining dully off its pitted tin roof. The night was not warm for early May, but no smoke issued from the stovepipe.

The room inside was dark and sparc and unkempt. Daniel lay awakc on the cot, his head tilted back against the wall behind him. A swath of pale moonlight shone through the bare paneless window. He stared out into the night woods, listless and vacant as if listening to something that wasn't there. His breath came thick, his eyes drooping hooded and heavy lidded. His three-day whiskers by now stiff dark bristles. Propped in the crook of his arm a lidless mason jar with two fingers of clear corn whiskey left in the bottom.

From somewhere off in the woods came the haunted call of an owl. He listened for a moment. The deep hooting voice came again and then fell silent. He lifted his head slightly up off the cot and replied.

"Hooo—"

He listened into the silence.

"Hooo—"

No other sound came. He let his head fall back against the wall and closed his eyes.

It was well past first light when the rumble of the trucks reached the camp. Early mist still hung on the hill slopes, veiling the blossoming trees. A waning half-moon faded in the morning sky. The birds were in full chorus but soon the noise of the engines and the grind of tires on gravel buried their voices. The guards stood outside the night shack leaning on their shotguns and blinking in the pale daylight. They watched the trucks pull around the hillside and stop in a line along the road, killing their engines. The men came off the truck beds moving slowly. They started walking down toward the mine along the coal-stained rails.

The last few men were going underground when a shape came out of the haze on the hill slope. Daniel appeared up the mountain walking down out of the woods. He wore a long john shirt and his miner's cap, his suspenders hanging down from his waist. He stepped out of the trees into the cinders and walked out in the middle of the lot. He was clearly drunk and stank of corn mash and unwashed coal miner. He threw his cap down in the gravel. His voice echoed through the camp.

"I tell you what, I'm ready to work! You hear me? I'll out-dig any man up here!"

He stood in the road, legs wide apart, breathing steam into the cold air.

"There aint none of you all can touch me—There aint a man left up here can outwork me—"

Joe came out onto the porch of the company house, looking around to see what was going on. The two guards started down from the shack at the top of the road to investigate the noise. They carried shotguns. Back in the office David came to the window and watched through the slits of the blinds.

Joe came off the porch of the company house still in shirtsleeves and stood at the foot of the steps. His face and neck flushed red. He turned and roared at the guards, hoarse and furious.

"Get this man off the property! I want him gone right now!"

He turned and glared at Daniel.

"You're fired, mister. If you show your face up here again, I'll put the law on you."

The two guards approached Daniel, slow and cautious, shotguns up. Daniel wheeled on them and struck an aggressive pose. He planted his boots in the gravel. They stopped and hesitated a moment, watching him. They could hear his breath coming heavy and thick.

One of them moved warily toward him. Daniel was too drunk to stand against him and staggered back. The guard stepped forward and swung the butt of his shotgun and caught Daniel good. The stock of the weapon slammed into his temple and blood spilled out of the gash. Daniel dropped to his knees, sucking air through his clenched teeth. He pressed his hands over his eyes and the blood seeped through his fingers.

So much blood came out of him it didn't look real. Even through the moonshine numb he rocked and seethed with the pain. Dust clung to the blood running down his neck, dyeing his pale long johns shirt deep red. A urine stain darkened his trouser leg. Holding their shotguns one-handed, the guards grabbed him under the arms. They dragged him off kicking and panting, trailing a bloody spoor in the dust.

Up in the office, still standing at the slatted blinds, David dropped his eyes and looked away.

Joe shook his head in disgust and cursed and spat in the dirt. He turned and walked back toward the company house, looking up at the office window.

20

I stood waiting with David at the altar, looking into the sunlight that flooded through the open doors at the far end of the church hall. The only other light came from the high windows and the panes of stained glass set along the walls, lending the sacrament the depth of shadow. All the guests stood looking back over their shoulders toward the doors. The organ produced a deep solemn music from its crib in the loft. The air in the church was sultry and close, but a breeze moved through the room that cooled us and made the almond-shaped candle flames tremble on the altar.

Two shadows walking arm in arm appeared outside in the churchyard. They stepped over the threshold into the nave and remained silhouettes until they began to pass through shafts of light alternating with darker regions along the aisle. Angeline had a chain of white daisies braided into her hair like a crown. She wore a simple ivory dress and carried a bouquet of bright wildflowers. Her sister's husband escorted her down the aisle.

She was backlit, so that for us her face remained in shadow, but the brilliant piece of day behind her caught in the lacy fabric of her dress, casting her in a gauzy glow. Her hair was swept back from her shoulders, the clean line of her neck curving against the light. As she approached I could even see the fine blonde down lit on her bare arms and the lovely smooth skin of her face.

She left her escort at the last pew and stood next to David. There were only a dozen people there, all sitting in the first several pews in front of the rail. Joe stood back behind David, looking uncomfortable in a suit. Angeline's sister was there as her witness. The groom and bride turned toward me. The organ stopped and there was a hush. I opened the book and read.

Behold, thou art fair, my love; behold thou art fair;
Thou hast doves' eyes.
Behold thou art fair, my beloved, yea, pleasant:
Also our bed is green.
The beams of our house are cedar,
And our rafters of fir.
Set me as a seal upon thine heart,
As a seal upon thine arm:
For love is strong as death;
Jealousy is cruel as the grave:
The coals thereof are coals of fire,
Which hath a most vehement flame.
Many waters cannot quench love,
Neither can the floods drown it:
If a man would give all the substance of his house for love,
It would utterly be contemned.

I began reciting the vows and they each repeated them. When they had both said till death do us part I called for the ring and

David took it out of his waistcoat pocket and pushed the gold band onto her finger. I said what God has joined here today let no man put asunder and he lifted the veil and they clasped hands and leaned together in a lingering kiss.

When they parted there was applause and the organ played. Some of the women were crying but Angeline herself remained composed. Everyone came forward and kissed and embraced them and gave them their warmest congratulations. Angeline's sister stood back with her husband, watching them and smiling. The couple walked back down the aisle and the guests filed out and followed them toward the doors.

I stood at the top of the steps outside, shaking hands with guests as they emerged into the daylight. The valley was incredibly green. Tiny wisps of milkweed and dandelion floated in the light, suspended in the heat. The maples moved in the breeze showing their silver underleaves.

David and Angeline walked out into the field. They stood under a dogwood in full bloom while a man took their picture. When they came back people stood on either side of the path and threw rice over them as the couple ducked and smiled. David opened the door of the black car and she climbed inside. He closed it behind her and walked around and got in behind the wheel. He leaned in the seat and called to us.

"All right now, everybody is invited on back to the house," he said. "We'll see you all up there."

He reached over and squeezed her hand, then turned the engine. The car coughed and fell in gear. She waved as he let out the brake and they rolled forward.

In the woods on the hillside across from the church Daniel stood back, concealed in the trees. The purple and black welt of a fresh-scabbed wound ran across his temple and back into the scalp, buried in his dark hair. Down the hillside the black car turned and drove off along the dirt road. He watched until it disappeared behind the trees.

PART III

21

We all stood out in the field around tables draped with immaculate white cloths. Everyone was talking and drinking ruby-colored punch ladled out of cut glass bowls. The sun was almost vertical and the rose-tinted streamers at the corners of the tables danced in the breeze. In the shade of the porch a trio of guitar, fiddle and mandolin struck up a country waltz that drifted out sad and sweet in the spring afternoon.

David and Angeline stood together as people came by and kissed them and shook their hands. They looked relaxed and happy, smiling with the guests. Without looking at her, he found her hand and held it as they greeted people. Now and then someone asked her for a dance in the field and she'd smile and accept. She stepped out in the grass, turning with her partner to the melancholy air of the waltz. David watched her movements out of the corner of his eye as he greeted the next guest.

After he'd said hello to everyone he came over and shook my hand.

"Congratulations," I said.

"Thank you, Father. Thanks for officiating."

"I wish the two of you well."

"You seem a bit pensive," he said. "Over here by yourself."

I nodded vaguely, gazing past the people as they stood and talked around the punch bowl. Beyond them along the edge of the field the black oaks and sugar maples stirred in the wind. I glanced back at him.

"I heard about what happened up at the camp," I said. "With John Black's brother. Pretty hard treatment for an old boy that was just up there drunk. Things haven't been especially easy on him lately. Did he really deserve all that?"

He studied me for a second and then he quoted:

"Use every man after his desert," he said, "and who shall scape whipping?"

When the train pulled into Charleston station it was late afternoon. David had been dozing against the window. When he opened his eyes she was holding his arm and watching him. She smiled and squeezed his hand.

"Wake up," she said. "We're here."

He blinked his eyes. "I feel better."

"Didn't you sleep last night?"

"I was up late with nerves."

They came down the steps of the passenger car and stood on the platform waiting for the conductor to open the baggage compartment. The engine's pneumatic brakes let out a steady hiss. The porters started unloading suitcases onto wheeled carts. They found the bags and followed their porter through the station lobby out to the taxi stand. They found a cab and David asked for the Charleston Hotel.

When they arrived the driver got out and went to the back of the car and opened the trunk. David stepped onto the curb and took Angeline's hand as she climbed out. He paid the driver, and the bellman was already carrying their bags inside. They checked in and went up in the elevator.

The bellman opened the door to the suite. In vases around the room were pale roses the color of blushing white skin. The porter brought in their luggage and David tipped him and thanked him. She stopped in the doorway and looked around the room. He stood behind her and smiled and put his arms around her shoulders.

He sat up in bed reading *Collier's* while she got ready. He listened to the sound of the running water in the bathroom echo against the porcelain and tile. When she opened door he could smell the water and the clean perfume of bath powder. She came out in a robe and dressed behind the changing screen in the corner of the room. She stepped out from behind the screen in a pale blue dress with her straight chestnut hair down to her shoulders. He glanced over from the bed and laid the magazine down open on his lap and looked at her.

"My God, you are beautiful," he said.

She smiled and her eyes fell away. She went back into the bathroom without saying anything but he could tell she was happy.

He got up and showered and changed his suit and put on a fresh shirt and collar. They went downstairs to the hotel dining room and stood at the door waiting to be seated. He watched her looking into the enormous room at the high ceilings, the crystal chandeliers and lace curtains.

"What do you think?"

"It's big," she said.

The maitre d'hôtel came up smiling to lead them back among the tables.

Night had already fallen when they left the hotel. The streets were still wet from a passing cloudburst. She took his arm and they walked without an umbrella. A warm breeze carried the sweet electric scent of ozone and low clouds moved in the sky behind the shadows of the buildings. In the air the smell of wet concrete and the hiss of automobiles passing on the damp asphalt. The green and red reflections of traffic lights blurred in the dark film of water on the street.

Down the street they could see the theater marquee shining in white, gold and red. Cars were pulling up along the curb and valets hustled to take them away. A loose column of men and women waited at the box office. They stood close together in line and watched the people, men in dark suits with squared-off pocket handkerchiefs and women in colorful spring dresses with gloves and stylish hats. They got their tickets and followed the peopled filing past the ticket taker.

Inside the crowd was milling around the lobby before the performance. The carpet was a deep pomegranate red. The chandeliers suspended from the ceiling on gilded chains cast their full brilliant light. The air smelled of perfume and tobacco smoke. All the voices merged in an excited hum. Men were smoking cigarettes and holding their hats while women gestured and smiled as they talked, their handsome faces shining under the light.

Angeline noticed a man standing inside the window. He wore a dark suit and hat. He was turned away from them, smoking a cigarette and looking out into the street. He moved so that she could see his profile against the dark window. He looked like John. She watched him. The man turned and walked out of the theater. He stopped in the street under the light of the marquee. He threw the cigarette down on the asphalt, black and slick with rain. Then he walked off and disappeared into the night.

She felt the blood rush out of her head and she put out her hand to steady herself. David took her arm and looked at her. She was pale and shaken.

"What's wrong?"

"I thought I saw a ghost," she said.

He put his arm around her shoulders and pulled her to him. He could feel her body shuddering.

"There are more things in heaven and earth," he said, leading her away from the crowd toward the door of the darkened auditorium.

When the play was over the house lights came up and they moved through the lobby out onto the sidewalk. The crowd was dissolving into the night. Men were standing at the edge of traffic trying to hail taxis. The valets had started pulling cars around in a line that stretched to the end of the block. Under the marquee lights the cars were slick and shiny with beaded rainwater.

They started walking back toward the hotel. She took his arm.

"Are you cold?"

"I'm all right," she said.

"What did you think of the play?"

"That was something."

"Did you like it?"

"I did," she said. "Very much. It was beautiful and very sad. I had a strange feeling when it was over though. Like I was exhausted and drained empty. But it felt good."

He nodded and put his arm around her shoulders and she leaned into him. They turned the corner and walked under the streetlamps. Away from the theater the streets were empty. A solitary cab passed them going the other way. Down the street the hotel rose up in front of them, its golden lights reflected in the rain slicked street. When they stepped under the lighted awning the doorman was there waiting to let them in.

They came in the darkened room. David closed the door behind them. He put his hands on her shoulders. She turned around and they stood close together facing each other. He touched her hair and she reached up and took his hand and kissed it and held it against her face. Then she moved his hand under hers and covered her breast. Feeling her body for the first time he leaned and kissed her. She opened herself and put her arms around him and pressed against him.

Light from the streetlamps below filtered in through the curtains pulled across the balcony doors. He could see her face. Her eyes were full and she was smiling. Her face glistened in the faint light, shining with tears of happiness and loss.

22

Angeline knelt in the eaves by the attic window and looked down into the field. It was still morning but the sun was already warming the roof shingles outside. The low room growing hot and close. The stale air smelled of raw pine and sawdust. Through the window the woods beyond the field were cool and green and shadowed. There was a truck backed into the gravel driveway below. Men were unloading the last pieces of furniture from the other house. She could hear Sarah's voice talking to them but she couldn't make out what was said.

She turned away from the window and wiped the dust from a small trunk. She undid the fasteners that were like buckles on either side of the front. Inside the trunk was a flat box of plain steel-gray metal. She opened the lid. Inside lay a bundle of letters bound with a faded ribbon. She took them out and held them in her lap. Underneath rested a rectangular picture frame wrapped in brown paper. She turned it over and gently undid the strips of tape that held the paper together. The loose paper unfolded and she felt the smooth edge of the frame inside and pulled it halfway out.

It was a picture of her first wedding. John stood in a dark suit and she held his arm. They were both smiling. She knelt there looking at it for a long moment. She touched the glass with her fingertips. There was a sound from somewhere down in the house. She closed the paper around the frame and opened the metal box and laid the picture inside. Then she covered it with the bundle of letters and closed the lid, laying the box down inside the trunk. She could hear the men coming up the stairs.

Angeline was in the kitchen when she heard the car roll up in the gravel. She heard the engine quit and the car door close. A minute later she heard the front door and David calling back into the house.

"Hello—"

"Back here," she called.

David appeared in the kitchen doorway, handsome in his dark suit and tie.

"You're off early."

"Sometimes I can sneak out," he said. "How was your first day?"

"Very good."

"It makes me happy to hear that," he said. "Where's Sarah?"

"Down in the cellar."

"Is everything all right?"

"What do you mean?"

"I was just a little worried—"

He trailed off, unsure.

She looked at him. "You mean about Sarah? Am I comfortable with her?"

"I suppose that's what I meant." He shook his head. "I don't know exactly."

He moved closer to her. He spoke in a low voice.

"Sarah's been with me a long time," he said. "I just want you to be happy here."

"I know. It's all right. Sarah is a lovely woman."

She turned toward the sink and absently touched the damp cloth on the edge of the basin.

"My parents died of the flu when I was sixteen," she said. "I went to Montgomery to live with my sister and her husband and finish school. When I graduated I didn't go to my ceremony. We couldn't afford the black shoes that went with the graduation gown. I got married that summer. We always worked hard to get by."

She looked at him again. "I'm just not accustomed to having any help."

Then she looked away and smiled and the tension was gone. "I think I can get used to it though," she said. She wiped her hands on her apron. "I just hope she doesn't mind me being here."

David watched her. "This is your place," he said.

She looked up into his eyes and smiled.

The room was dark. David could feel the shadows and the faint glow of the night sky. He felt the cool air coming in through the windows and the cool sheets. Against him the warm smoothness of her legs and her flank under the nightgown. He knew she was awake. He felt her breathing there beside him. He stared up into the dark. He moved his hand under the sheet and touched her smooth firm skin with his fingertips. He touched her legs and her slim arms and found her hand and lingered there. He didn't look at her when he spoke.

"I never thought I could have anything like this," he said, his voice low and even in the stillness of the room.

There was a long silence. He could feel her there next to him in the dark and his own heart softly beating.

David pulled up in front of the company house and parked the car. The early morning was overcast. Wisps of fog lingered on the mountainside. He did not see any lights in the office windows. When he tried the door it was locked. He looked in the window, shading his eyes to see into the darkened room. The office was empty. He came off the porch and started walking down the hill toward the mine. He looked back toward the road. The line of trucks empty and silent at the top of the hill.

He walked along the tracks running toward the tunnel mouth. There was no sign of anyone. He stopped and listened just outside the hole. The knock of mule's hooves echoed somewhere off in the dark. He moved into the passage and walked a little way along the tracks. His hand felt along the wall touching the cool rock. He thought he saw a flickering light up ahead. The faint noise of men working came from somewhere farther down.

"Hey boys—"

His voice echoed down the tunnel and died away. He stood and listened. There was a noise in the dark ahead of him. A man stepped out of the shadow into the faint light seeping in from the surface. He was in miner's overalls and cap, his face ashen in the shadow of the tunnel. It was John Black. David looked into his eyes and they were dark, emotionless holes.

"I need blood," he said.

David opened his eyes. The bedroom was silent and dark. Light from the night sky cast shadows onto the floor under the windows. Beside him in the bed Angeline was sleeping, her body moving faintly with every shallow breath.

When he woke up in the morning she was not there beside him. He turned over on his back and lay in bed. He heard her moving in the bathroom. There was the sound of water running and then he heard her throwing up. A second later she was sick again. He could hear the vomit splash against the porcelain and water.

"Are you all right?"

There was no answer. He got out of bed and stood outside the bathroom. The door was ajar and there was a sour smell. The water was running in the sink.

"Can I come in?"

"I'm all right," she said from behind the door. "I must have eaten something bad."

Suddenly the veil of blossoms over the woods fell away, replaced by a dense emerald surge on the boughs. Boys pushed the bladed cylinders of mowers over thickening lawns and the smell of cut grass hung in the air, succulent and almost sweet. In the late afternoon I walked beyond the last houses down the path along the field. Wisteria hung in bloom along the trees, muted violet on the vine.

I started to come up the drive toward the house but I saw David out in the yard. Pale blue innocence flowers had transformed the field. He was leaning down in shirtsleeves clearing sticks and old pine cones out of the grass. He walked out to the edge of the woods and dumped what he was carrying into the underbrush. When he turned and started walking back toward the house he saw me and waved. I waved to him and we walked toward each other to a spot in the yard. We met and shook hands and grinned at each other.

"It's been a while," I said.

"Since the wedding."

"How are you?"

"I'm happy, Nathan. For once I can say that."

"Good," I said. "I like hearing it."

"I hope you plan to stay for supper. Angeline will want to see you."

"We might arrange that."

"Stay right here," he said. "There's something I want to show you."

He went to the house and left me standing in the field. When he came back out he was carrying a wooden case with a leather handle. He knelt down in the grass and opened the dark varnished cherry wood box. Nested in velvet cloth were a half dozen silver metal spheres engraved with two different geometric patterns. One set with concentric rings and the other with an interlocking design. In among them rested a smaller ball made of wood.

"Have you ever played?"

"I don't believe so," I said. "What exactly is it?"

"It's boules. The old-timers play it on Sunday afternoons up at the camp. I found the set at a shop in town."

He found a thin stick in the grass and laid it out as the pitching line. He handed me the small wooden target and told me to go ahead and toss it a ways out into the field. I pitched it underhand about a dozen yards out and he said that would do. We each took three of the fist-sized silver metal boules. He stood behind the line and eyed the target. I watched his motion, how he bent at the knee and let his arm swing several times as he lined up his aim. He let go a high, arching underhand toss and the boule dropped in the grass with a thud and rolled right up to the wooden ball, kissing it with a soft click. He turned and grinned at me.

"Not bad."

"Now you throw your first one," he said, "and whichever of us is closer gets to throw the rest of his. Then the other one tries to get his last two the closest or knock the other's away."

I threw mine and it rolled wide. Then he threw his last two and won. When we finished the game he said he'd be back and went in the house. He came back with a flask of bourbon and a bowl of ice and two glasses. I watched him as he stood on the porch. He mixed two drinks and then came back out into the field.

We stood for a minute drinking the whiskey and ice, then we put the glasses down in the grass and started another game. He lined up to throw.

He spoke without looking at me. "What is your understanding of the forgiveness of mortal sin?"

I glanced at him. "You want my official opinion?"

"Well, it is your area."

He threw and we watched his boule roll close to the target. I stared out at the pattern of silver balls in the grass. For a moment I considered what he had asked.

"If a man is penitent in his heart," I said, "and receives the sacrament of confession, there is no sin that can't be redeemed."

I gripped the boule and lined up to throw. "Though the penance may be dear," I said, aiming.

I pitched and the metal ball fell and rolled in the grass and knocked his boule away from the target.

23

On the last evening of spring the night breeze came in sweet and cool through the open window of the bedroom. David could taste in the air the first hint of the lush, redolent smell of summer's full verdure. He lay across the bed and closed his eyes, letting the night air soothe his temples. He inhaled deeply and opened his eyes.

He sat up and took off his shoes. He stood and took his jacket off the bed and hung it in the closet and undid his necktie and collar and took off his shirt. He stood in his undershirt and trousers and rubbed his eyes.

Angeline came out of the bathroom in her nightgown. She sat down on the edge of the bed and watched him get undressed.

"I think I'd like to go and see Dr. Perry," she said.

He stopped and looked at her. "Are you still feeling bad?"

"No," she said. "Not all the time." Her eyes fell away. "I just want to make sure everything is all right."

"I'll call him right now," he said. "I'll find out if he can see you first thing in the morning. Is that all right?"

"Yes. That would be fine."

"Tomorrow is Saturday, but I don't think he would mind too much."

He sat down on the bed beside her and put his arm around her and kissed her forehead. She leaned into him and took his hand.

"Poor honey."

"I'm all right," she said.

"I'll go call him right now."

"All right."

In the morning David waited for her downstairs in the kitchen. He sat at the table drinking coffee. Sarah stood at the stove frying an egg. When Angeline came into the room Sarah turned around and gave her a worried look.

"Can I fix you something, dear?"

"I don't think I could eat anything. Thank you though."

"How about a cup of coffee with milk?"

"I could take a little coffee," she said. "Thank you."

Sarah poured her a cup of coffee and set it on the table with the milk. Angeline sat down and smiled bleakly at David. He tried to give her a reassuring look. When he finished his coffee he touched her hand as he got up from the table. He went in the other room and got his hat and came back and stood in the kitchen doorway. He looked at Sarah.

"We'll be back in a couple of hours."

"I'll be here," she said.

The morning was warm and bright. The ice truck was coming around and the sun glinted off the ice in the open bed like blocks of wet glass. The magnolias were all in bloom and as they drove through town they looked back among the houses and saw children retreating into a fastness of white blossoms.

Angeline was quiet and he reached over in her lap and found her hand. She gazed off along the running road, watching the stippled landscape. When she closed her eyes she could still feel the morning sunlight beyond her eyelids flickering through the trees as the car drove past.

The doctor's house was set back from the road on a rutted dirt drive. They turned in and pulled up along the stone-paved walk. The engine died and he came around and took her hand as she stepped out of the car. Dr. Perry's wife stood in the screen door as they came up the steps. She took Angeline's hand and leaned forward and kissed her cheek and then turned her face up and kissed David lightly.

"It's good to see you all. I wish you'd come down and visit us sometime."

"We mean to, Laura," he said. "Once we're all settled in."

"All right then."

They came in the house and she took his hat and turned to Angeline.

"The office is right through there, dear."

Angeline glanced at David uncertainly.

"It's all right," Mrs. Perry said. "He's expecting you."

David touched her arm. "I'll be right here," he said.

They watched her go back into the other room. The doctor's wife turned and smiled at David.

"Now what can I fix you?"

◆ ◆ ◆

The doctor kept an office in the back of the house. There was an anteroom like a parlor that was lined with bookshelves and dark paintings of horses and ships. David sat on the sofa under the window and looked at a magazine. Mrs. Perry came in with a cup of tea on a saucer and set it down on the low table. He looked up from the magazine and she gave him a comforting smile.

"Thanks, Laura."

"You're welcome."

She went back out of the room and he raised the hot tea to his mouth and inhaled the deep flavor of the steam but he didn't drink any. He looked at the photographs in the magazine. A few minutes later the door opened and Angeline came out followed by Dr. Perry. He had his hand on her shoulder and he was talking to her in his low voice.

David stood up. "Is everything all right?"

The doctor grinned at him. "Congratulations," he said. "Angeline is going to have a baby."

David looked at her. She was smiling. She slid under his left side and pressed against him. He reached over with his free arm and shook hands with Dr. Perry

"Thank you, Cy."

"My great pleasure," the doctor said, still grinning at them.

Dr. Perry walked them to the front porch and his wife came out as they were leaving and made them promise again that they'd come soon for a social visit. They thanked them both again and Mrs. Perry smiled and embraced Angeline. David shook the doctor's hand one last time and they came down off the porch waving.

He held the car door for her and she climbed in and he waited and closed it behind her. He came around and got in behind the wheel and turned the engine. Angeline reached over and put her hand on his fist gripping the gear knob. He turned and looked at her. She was watching him.

"There's something I want you to do for me," she said.

She watched him. He smiled and she could see how happy he was.

"Anything," he said.

Toward noon David came down the hill into the trees. It was the longest day of the year. A sheen of sunlight flashed on the surface of the river, sending a shimmering pattern up through the trees. At the bottom of the slope he passed into a region of shadow under the canopy of leaves. The water beyond shed the strong cool smell of moss and rich silt.

He looked out into the sun along the bank. The river shone green and blue. A figure stood in the rocks, fishing off the riverbank. David stopped at the edge of the trees and watched him. Down the bank a bale of turtles were sunning themselves on the rocks at the edge of the water. Their shells were dull purple and black. They stretched out their leathery necks and looked back toward the trees. He stepped forward into the clearing. It was warm in the sun and beneath him the dark cobbles held the midday heat. A turtle slid silently off the rocks and disappeared into the river.

David's voice broke the silence.

"Are they alive?"

Daniel turned and looked. By now his beard was full and dark with ruddy hints around the mouth. The hair at his neck nearly touched his collar. The pale line of a scar faded into the skin at his temple. He watched David for a moment, holding his line in the water. He turned back toward the river without saying anything. David took a few steps out in the rocks toward him.

"I came down here to talk to you."

Daniel gazed out on the water. He held the pole still. The line moved faintly in the current. David stood watching him.

"There's no reason we have to be at odds," David said.

His voice was conciliatory, but the words seemed to drift off down the river without effect. He wasn't even sure if Daniel had heard him. He took a few steps out toward the edge.

"You've been out of work a month now. I know it hasn't been easy. I might be able to speak to Joe on your behalf. Get you back on a probationary basis."

David waited for him to speak. The younger man didn't even look up from the water.

"You don't have to make things this hard on yourself," David said finally.

There was a long silence. Daniel stood motionless, his line sending out rings on the smooth surface of the water. He never looked at David. He kept watching the river as if he had not heard him. David waited, until he thought that he wasn't going to speak at all. He shook his head and was almost ready to turn away.

"I'm already past all that," Daniel said, still not looking at him, just staring out at the water.

David studied him a long moment. He started to speak again but didn't. He turned and walked back into the trees.

24

When he pulled up to the house he could see her out in the field. She had on a pale yellow dress and her face and arms were starting to copper in the sun. She turned and looked when she heard the car. David got out and waved and started walking to her. A pair of rooks gleaned in the yard.

He saw that she was laying out stakes for a new garden. A length of white string stretched in the grass, forming one long side of the plot along the edge of the woods. He leaned and kissed her, tasting the warm salt of her mouth. He touched her hair and her neck, sultry and damp with sweat. She pointed along invisible boundaries in the ground.

"Late beans next week," she said. "And corn and carrots the week after."

"How are you feeling?"

"I'm all right. It gets better in the afternoon."

"Can I convince you to come out of this heat?"

"Might do."

They left the wire stakes and the ball of string in the grass and walked back toward the house. The sun was almost vertical. A hush hung over the heat-stunned day. They came up into the shade of the porch and sat down on the steps. A column of black ants filed along the edge of the steps, disappearing into a crack between two boards. David gazed out into the field.

"I found him down by the river."

"What did he say?"

He shook his head vaguely. "I don't think he's interested in my help."

Angeline looked at him bleakly. She didn't say anything.

In the evening they lay together in the dark of the summer dusk with the air coming in warm and faint like a continuous breath. The hum and murmur of the insects lulled them on the edge of sleep. David turned over and looked at her. She was awake, the faint light limning her face, her eyes shining in the dark. Their bodies were close under the sheet and he moved his arm and rested it against her flank. Breathing deeply, he closed his eyes again and tried to drift off.

He could feel her there beside him, tense and awake. He opened his eyes again and looked at her. She was staring off in the dark.

"I was pregnant once before," she said.

For a moment he was silent. He reached under the sheet in the dark and found her hand.

"It's all right," he said softly. "It's going to be all right."

At dawn the river smoked dark like molten glass. From somewhere came the first plaintive rasp of ducks. A fisherman walked down out of the mist to the shore. An old rowboat was pulled up on the bank with its oars lying inside the hull across the boards. He laid his rod in the boat and pushed alongside it in the sand, launching it out from the bank. After a few strokes he lifted the oars and the boat drifted out into the river. He took his pole and baited the hook. He sat in silence, casting into the dull mirror of the water and letting the boat drift.

Toward noon he came up through the trees to the back porch of the house with a dozen trout strung through their mouths on a wire. Braced and lying flat in the crook of a low tree branch near the house was a board nailed into the wood like a shelf. The wire had a fastener like a clip and he hung it from a nail in the board leaving the fish suspended there. The bellies of the trout were pale, shading darker along their flanks toward the deep gold back scales.

He undid the clasp and lifted the first trout and laid it on the board. With his knife he slit the fish open and pulled the pink guts out onto the wood. A strong clean smell rose from its insides. The gills glistened in the sunlight, crimson and plantlike. He tossed the entrails in the weeds, leaving the board stained with oily blood.

On a nail driven into the tree itself hung a rusty steel tool like a pair of rude pliers. He laid the fish flat and started to scrape the scales from its metallic flanks with the sharp edge of the tool. The silvery fish scales scattered as he worked, glittering down among the blades of grass. He laid the dressed trout in a wicker creel and took the next one from the wire. When he'd finished cleaning the trout he hung the scraper back on the nail. He wiped his knife clean on his trouser leg and walked up toward the house with the creel.

◆ ◆ ◆

On the Fourth of July a brass band played in the field by the town hall. People stood in the shade listening to the patriotic marches in the afternoon heat. Boys gathered in the dust at the edge of the field. A circle was drawn in chalk on the packed earth and they crowded around its perimeter kneeling and leaning to look. The marbles gleamed blue and green, gold and rose in the ruddy sunlight. The boys leaned and shot and the beads settled in patterns like constellations in the dust. Every shot meant the loss or gain of a marble and was marked with sharp breathy exclamations. When the band paused between numbers you could hear the dull click of glass striking glass.

Angeline came down the road toward the park. She stopped at the edge of the field and took off her shoes. Her blue dress, hat and shoes were not fancy or extravagant, but obviously new. She walked barefoot in the grass along the trees toward the town hall. There was an empty bench in the shadow of a black oak and she sat watching the spectacle in the humid afternoon. The light gleaming on the brass of the instruments, the band in straw hats against the white, shaded side of the town hall, the children waving sparklers in the field. She closed her eyes and listened to the music and the murmur of the crowd. The deep beat of the tuba pushed the horns forward in a finale that grew to a crescendo and flourish and left everyone breathless.

For a while after the band had stopped playing she sat and watched the children chase each other in the grass. Finally the musicians finished packing their instruments and disappeared into the town hall. People followed them inside or gradually drifted away. She got up and put her shoes on and started walking back through the grass. Across the field several ladies watched her with veiled looks until she turned her back to go, then stared openly. They leaned their heads together and whispered as she passed behind the houses.

In the evening they came down to the river. The air was thick, warm, and fragrant. The pale yellow trumpets of jewelweed decorated the deep green undergrowth along the bank. In the dusk the last fisherman came up the slope and waved to them. Slung over his shoulder a wicker creel hung on a strap. He grinned at them in the grainy light and held up his rod and tackle and called out, you all need to come on up to the house. Through the trees they could see the party lights strung along under the eaves of the back porch.

Fireflies started to glow, their phosphorescent bodies rising in the twilight. They walked along the undergrowth plucking honeysuckle blossoms, pulling them open and tasting the drops of sugary nectar with their tongues. The subtle down that spread under the petals and lined the soft undersides of the blossoms was the same new velvet that in the deep woods thickened on the antlers of deer.

They sat under the evening sky and he could smell the strong menthol of camphor she always rubbed on her wrists to keep off mosquitoes. He kissed her and tasted the cool sweet salt of her mouth. They were joined in silhouette against the water luminous with moonlight. They watched the animate shadows of birds and saw dark rings spreading in the water where fish kissed the surface. Angeline stood along the bank under the dusk and moved in slow elegant imitation of a blue heron hunting the shallows of the river.

When they started up the hill toward the house they could hear the voices on the porch. People were gathering for the party. The fisherman had a shallow kettle full of pale gold oil over a flame, starting to boil. He took the filets and rolled them in flour and dipped them quickly in cornbread batter and dropped them in the oil. He scooped them out into a basket lined with brown paper to soak up the grease. The air had the savory taste of trout fried in batter.

Women came out of the house with bowls of cool potato salads and slaw. A girl sat over a board slicing potatoes into wedges for frying. A woman in the grass nearby turned ice cream in a tub filled with ice and salt.

By then it was fully dark and the old men abandoned throwing horseshoes in the yard. Under the blue glow of the party lights someone was tuning a guitar and another drew the bow of a fiddle over strings that buzzed dissonant and gradually bent into key. People started to come by with pans of cornbread, a few stoppered bottles of homemade beer, and mason jars full of clear corn whiskey.

They walked up through of the yard onto the back porch. David shook the white floured hand of the man frying fish. Angeline leaned down and kissed the woman turning the ice cream on the cheek and took her hand. A banjo and mandolin joined the combo and the band struck up a bluegrass tune. The guitar thrummed in the bottom of the music, the banjo and mandolin ran antic, and the lonesome voices of the men sang in sad refrain.

That night there were fireworks over the river. The rockets burst red, gold, and blue, their flashes illuminating the trees, doubled in the dark mirror of the water.

25

At the end of August the world was still in the late afternoon. The house stood silent in the heat. Goldenrod swayed in the faint breeze along the edge of the field. Daisies and clover grew thick on the verge of the woods. The new garden throve under an absolute sun. Stalks of late corn cased in thick emerald shucks stood waist high in serried rows, and the green hairs of carrots veiled the soil. Tomatoes drooped ripe, heavy and red. A yard-wide strip of ground lay freshly turned, waiting for peas, celery, and late kale.

Angeline came out of the house and walked toward the woods at the farthest corner of the field. Three whitewashed hives stood there in the grass. She'd set them up the month before and the bees had taken, but now something new was happening. She scanned the trees along edge of the woods a few yards away. She studied the mottled bark flecked with lichen.

In the crook of a sapling's branch they were swarming. She stood and watched them. The bees clambered over themselves and shivered in a clotted globe. They moved innumerable, mysterious and hypnotic, a vague enigma. They seemed to vibrate and throb with some desultory impulse, coalesced there to form some other, threshold creature hanging liminal at the edge of nature. She watched a few of them dance their frantic, trembling language to the rest of the shifting mass. She wondered what power moved them. She thought that if she could find the queen and kill her they might return to the hive. Finally she decided just to let them go.

She went to the garden and looked at the corn, absently pulling a few weeds. Somewhere distant she heard faint music. It floated vague and ghostly over the valley. She stood up in the garden and listened. After a moment she recognized the carnival wheeze of the calliope coming up the river.

A thrill spread through town and by nightfall everyone was on their way down to the water. The stern-wheel showboat had moored off the bank and extended a long gangplank down to the shore. A small brass band immediately disembarked and marched straight into the middle of town and around the block. They stopped in the street by the post office and played a medley. Everyone came out to look. When they'd finished they struck up another tune and turned and marched back toward the river, their music fading away down the hill.

All afternoon and into the evening, ever since the calliope had first announced its arrival, children had been begging their mothers to be taken down to see the beautiful white vessel, gilded and brilliant. The ship stood gleaming there, its smokestacks festooned with pennants that shifted in the wind, its great paddle wheel at rest half-submerged. The river lapped against the stern where its name was painted in big red letters, the *Elsinore.*

The evening brought some relief from the heat. A half moon hung in the dusk. Lamps winked on in the windows of houses and old men sat mute on front porches exhausted in shirtsleeves. Women called their children inside and hustled back in the kitchen, busy fixing something quick and provisional. Everyone was getting ready to go down to the water.

The showboat waited on the river and the town could feel its presence, fleeting and dreamlike. There was a carnival feeling in the air. People had saved all summer and now had a few nickels to spend. As the sun started to sink behind the mountains they were gradually drawn down to the water from every direction, converging on the showboat, following the gentle lilt of the calliope. Young couples walked arm in arm down the hill and women herded eager children with threats and promises, their minds wild with imagined delights.

David and Angeline passed beyond the last few houses and the lights of the town faded behind them as they walked into a stand of willow and sycamore. The road under them turned to rutted gravel of uncertain footing and then to a smooth hard dirt path running steep down the slope. The dense black boughs hung over them forming a shadowed passage. The air had the tang of evergreen and the vague decaying smell of the summer woods.

People hesitated in the dark, edging down along the path. They stumbled on and gradually the branches started to thin and separate. Now out past the verge of the woods they began to see some faint color. Beyond the trees the golden lights of the showboat were shining on the water.

The couple emerged from the trees, coming down the dirt path with the crowd. He walked just ahead and reached back for her hand as she followed, steadying her as she came. The boat shone there in the dark water like a vision. At the bottom of the path they entered the ring of light the vessel shed onto the bank.

Angeline was tawny from the sun and had on a green cotton summer dress. She was still slim, at three months not yet showing. David was pale and his dark hair shone in the light. He wore a dark blue suit without a tie. His collar was open at the neck, the white line of his undershirt showing. People ahead were already filing two abreast up the gangplank, disappearing onto the deck. They stopped at the edge and looked at the plank running up from the muddy bank to the ship like a steep bridge over the water. She took his arm and they started climbing the ramp.

Lamps hung on poles above the lacquered deck, gleaming dark and sleek. People stood silhouetted in line buying tickets at a booth. Beyond them warm light poured out through the open doors of the entry hall. The calliope had stopped and they could hear other music coming from inside. They stepped up to the booth and David slid two dimes onto the counter. The coins gleamed in the lamplight and the girl took them and slid back two tickets. At the threshold a man tore them into stubs and they entered the brightly lit hall.

Inside everything was ornate, embellished with baroque carving or swaddled in plush fabrics. Tassels edged dark velvet draperies. Children dragged their mothers from one marvel to the next, gaping at the paintings and gilded mirrors. In one corner a man at an upright piano produced a lively rag while a drummer beat time on bass and snare. A juggler stood out in the middle of the floor in a straw hat and suspenders tossing bowling pins and grinning at the crowd. People lined up at the vending carts, inhaling the warm taste of corn popping in oil and peanuts roasting that flavored the atmosphere.

The doors of the theater opened and two ladies appeared in pale lacy dresses and painted faces. They were twin sisters and they came over and stood by the piano. The man started a sad jazz and the drummer hung his head and caressed the snare with wire brushes. The ladies sang a languid ballad in harmony, drawling the sentimental lyric out in long lilting phrases. When the song ended they curtsied and smiled to polite applause and then disappeared back from where they had come.

The theater doors stood open. People drifted inside eating popcorn and staring at the curtained stage and the rows of empty seats and the curving balconies. The evening's play was not set to start for another half an hour but a woman was already settling her children along a row of seats while they begged her to let them sit in the balcony.

The entrance music started again in the hall and people began to drift away, milling around the passages that ran the length of the boat. David and Angeline walked through the passages, looking at the games and exhibits set up in kiosks like a little carnival. They stood in a small crowd watching a man toss darts at a wall of balloons. A hawker came by with a tray of roasted peanuts in paper bags and David bought one. They wandered further along the corridor absently shucking peanuts and watching the people leaning into the different booths with their children.

Down at the end of the hall the crowd thinned out. They could still hear the faint music and underneath it the vague murmur of the people. There were no more booths, just a display table selling bottled tincture of black walnut hull and wormwood, the dark glass gathering dust in wooden cases and shining dully in the lamplight. The barker there told them it was good for any parasite whatsoever but they just smiled politely and shook their heads and moved on.

At the very end of the corridor was a door marked by a placard illustrated with tarot cards and the signs of the zodiac. A heavy purple velvet curtain hung across, covering the doorway. They studied the sign. Its edges were worn and the color of the gilded lettering faded.

She looked at him.

"Go ahead," he said. "It's all right. We have time."

Angeline hesitated and then parted the curtain and stepped inside. It was dimly lit and it took a moment for her eyes to adjust. In the middle of a small room a woman sat behind a circular table, the only light from a few candles burning on low shelves. Gilded things gleamed in the candle glow on the dark cloth spread over the table. In the dim air the lingering musk and spice of incense. The woman smiled and indicated for her to sit. Her eyes were dark gems.

Angeline smiled back shyly. She stepped forward and sat down across the table. The woman looked at her gravely and spoke in a mock-serious voice.

"Is this your first time?"

Angeline smiled. "Yes," she said.

"Just relax, sweetheart. Clear your mind."

The woman took the deck in her hands.

"I'm going to ask you to pick some cards," she said.

Angeline smiled, closed her eyes and took a deep breath.

David wandered down the hall looking at the different booths. The attractions seemed somewhat run down but people were enjoying the diversion immensely, especially the children. He stood and watched two boys at a booth throwing wooden rings over the tops of bottles trying to win little prizes. They didn't win anything. He stepped up and handed the man running the game a quarter.

"One more round," he said.

The man gave him a big handful of the rings and he smiled at the boys and divided the rings between the three of them. They started taking turns tossing at the bottles.

The woman spread out a dozen cards face down between them on the cloth. They were worn and stained and large, the size of a man's hand. Their backs marked with a dark, elaborate pattern. As she slowly turned them over one by one they showed beautiful hand-painted images, each one unique. Gilded pictures stylized like ikons showing strange and dramatic scenes. Hanged men, swords, lovers, and skulls appeared as she reversed the cards.

Angeline smiled with the thrill and romance of having her fortune told. The woman seemed pleased as she explained the meaning of the patterns. She gestured, indicating a series of pictures. She dealt three more cards and turned the first. It showed golden bowls bounded by pomegranates, lotus blossoms, and flowing water.

"Ah," she said. "Three of cups. Signifying love and abundance."

The woman smiled knowingly. Angeline flushed red in the candlelight.

The woman turned another card. Her face darkened as if she saw something that disturbed her. She hesitated, and Angeline instantly knew something was wrong.

Angeline smiled hesitantly. "What is it?"

The fortune-teller tried to smile at her reassuringly. She quickly composed herself, turning the next card.

"Nothing dear," she said.

26

The deep woods blushed on the first day of autumn, still mottled green but limned now with ruddy color. The play of September hues shifted on the mountains, rich and vivid. Gold and ocher, umber and rust. Scarlet firepink flowers studded the undergrowth. The sun had burned away the morning clouds and hung now brilliant in the blue afternoon. It quickened the sap in the knotted limbs of the maples, full of the sugars that would feed them until spring.

Daniel sat on a stump in an open glade clear of brush. The shanty leaned behind him in the trees. He balanced a busted axe on his knees, trying to fix the blade to the haft with a rusted nail and a scrap of wire. He wore an old plaid flannel shirt hanging open over long johns discolored by a faded bloodstain, ruddy brown on the pale dingy underwear. His dark trousers riddled with coarse stitching. A shotgun leaned on a log nearby.

There was a sound down along the path. He looked up, scanning the trees.

Angeline appeared back in the woods. She walked up through the trees, wearing a plain blue dress and the same old worn brown brogans. He watched her approach. Blank and impassive, his face caged behind his eyebrows and dark beard.

She came up and stood before him. He sat on the decaying stump like some ragged backwoods king on his throne.

"I've been meaning to come up and see you," she said apologetically.

She paused, waiting for him to respond. He glanced at her but didn't speak. He tinkered with the axe.

"You look thin," she said. "Have you been all right?"

She looked at his hands, his cracked and blackened fingernails. His haggard manner. The overpatched clothes hung loose on his gaunt body. He had been out of work the whole three months of summer, trading the ginseng he gathered along the hollows for cornmeal and corn whiskey. Drinking white lightning and living off roots, nuts, and wild game. He looked half-wild himself, his whiskers thick and bristling, his dark hair combed back in its own grease.

When he spoke it was in a low still voice, hardly audible. The expression on his face barely altered.

"I saw you get married," he said.

"Why didn't you come in?"

"I saw it the first time."

There was a silence. For a moment she watched him. She reached into the pocket of her dress and held out a handful of folded bills.

"Here—"

He looked at the money.

"I want you to have this."

He looked off into the woods.

"I don't need your company money," he said. His voice was bitter and hard. "Everything I need, I got right here. You got what you need now."

A silence divided them. His words hung there hurtful and derisive. His eyes fell away and he gazed down at the broken axe in his lap. His torn and blackened hands.

"Go on," he said finally. "I don't want to see you up here no more."

She held the money out a moment longer. Then she let it drop to her side. She stood there with the bills wadded in her fist, staring at him beseeching and sad.

Finally she seemed to wilt slightly in defeat. Her shoulders dropped and she gave the faintest sigh. She turned and slowly walked off back into the woods, looking back once. He never got up from the stump. His scarred and callused hands lingered over the dead metal of the axe head. He watched her disappear back down the path.

In the late afternoon a lone hunter stalked the woods somewhere down along the hollow. Daniel could hear him in the distance imitating the calls of birds. All else was still. The sun slanted down through the trees in cathedrals of shadow and light.

The shanty stood beyond in the cool of the glade. In the shadowed room Daniel sat on the edge of the cot by the window and stared out at the autumn mountainside. He listened to the faint calls of the hunter far off in the woods. He got up and went across the room to the old desk in the corner. He slid open the top drawer. Inside there was a tarnished case of battered gray steel. He touched the pitted metal, running his fingertips over the cold dull surface of the box.

That night after dinner Angeline went back in the kitchen and helped Sarah clean up. The two women worked in silence, tired from the day and preoccupied. David was in the parlor with his bourbon and cigars. In the kitchen the women could hear faint music drifting back through the house.

After Sarah had gone home Angeline stood in the empty kitchen and took off her apron and folded it. She turned out the downstairs lights except the porch lamp and locked the front door. She stopped in the hall by the parlor door and looked into the warmly lit room.

David sat by the fire in his armchair staring at the chessboard, the phonograph playing low in the corner. A cigar smoldered beside him in a glass ashtray. She stood half-shadowed in the darkened hall and listened to the music. The jazz had a sweet and melancholy air. She could smell the close heavy odor of his cigar. Finally she stepped into the light of the doorway.

"I'm going on upstairs."

He glanced up from the board and smiled absently.

"All right," he said. "I'm right behind you."

He stared back at the pieces. She stood in the doorway watching him.

"I went up there to see him," she said.

"Who?"

"Daniel. Up in the woods."

He turned and looked at her.

"When did you go up there?"

"Today. This afternoon. I was worried and I just wanted to see if he was all right."

She stepped forward into the room, still holding the apron. He watched her.

"I tried to give him some money but he wouldn't take it. I'm afraid he'll get sick and no one will know it. Nobody ever goes up there to see him."

She paused. David didn't say anything.

"I don't know what to do," she said. "He was like a brother to me and now he doesn't have anyone."

David looked back at the fire and shook his head. He got up out of the chair and came and stood by her and took her hand.

"Sweetheart, we've both tried. He doesn't want our help. He's got to go down his own road."

He touched her face and moved a loose wisp of hair away from her forehead.

"I want you to promise me you won't go up there again."

He watched her.

"Promise me."

She moved as if to speak but she stopped. Her eyes fell and she looked away. After a long moment she nodded and sighed.

"All right," she said. "I promise."

Yellowed pages of old newspaper covered the inner pane of the cellar window. From outside in the night only the faintest glow was visible of the fire that burned there underground.

The room itself was circled in shadow. In one corner a lamp shed dim, discolored light. The air was stagnant and close, the low cellar never meant for habitation. A damp subterranean smell rose from the packed earth floor. Along one wall a few dusty mason jars of green beans and stewed tomatoes lined a set of narrow shelves that were just bare boards. A set of raw pine stairs ran up to a door closed to the house above.

A cot had been brought down and arranged in one corner, a worn leather valise on the dirt floor beneath it. A night table and lantern. A pen scratched there in the pallid light. Mr. Wilkinson sat facing the wall. He leaned over a school desk that was too small for him, writing in the wan circle cast by the lamp.

The door opened at the top of the stairs and warm light from the kitchen above shone down into the cellar room. The silhouette of a woman appeared at the top of the stairs. She came down carrying a plate that steamed in the dank air. There was the smell of potatoes and baked ham. She stood by the desk, hesitating in the silence. She set the plate down on the corner of the desk with a knife and fork. He did not acknowledge her presence and kept writing.

She looked at him. "Here you go, Mr. Wilkinson."

The sound of the pen stopped and he glanced up, preoccupied from behind his spectacles. His glasses reflected the flat lamplight, giving his face a blank lifeless look. She stood there uncomfortable for a moment, then turned and went back up the stairs and closed the door behind her. He went back to the page without looking at the food. The pen began to scratch again in the silence.

◆ ◆ ◆

Toward the end of September I went up to visit Will again in the hospital. The autumn light fell in shafts through the tall windows. The long hall of the ward was clean and white. He was sitting up in bed reading. When he saw me he laid the book down face up on his lap and grinned. I came over and shook his hand and sat down in the chair by the bed. I glanced at the open page. He had been reading Job.

"I didn't know you could read, Will."

"Don't make me laugh, Father. I might not recover."

"How have you been?"

"I won't complain. The nurses would hear of it."

His breathing still came raspy and shallow, his voice broken with rheum, but he seemed more alive than he had in months.

"What are you reading there?"

He closed the book on his lap and showed me the cover.

"My present condition has set me thinking," he said. "It's about all I'm fit for."

He looked away and there was a silence. We sat there together for a moment without speaking, but there was no uncomfortable feeling. There was a peaceful quality about him that I liked. After a while he spoke again.

"Have you ever been deer hunting, Father?"

"No, I never have."

He stopped and considered.

"There's something to it," he said. "Not the shooting itself. There's something else that goes on."

"What is it?"

"I'm not sure I could say precisely. Some kind of exchange. I might even compare it to a sacrament."

"Like Mass?"

"Not exactly—"

He trailed off and stared for a second as if he were searching for the right word. Then he seemed to come back. He glanced at me again.

"I thought you might be interested," he said.

"I might be."

In the evening I drove up to the house. The sun had already gone behind the mountains when I came up the road and it was quickly getting dark. I pulled in the drive and the headlights of the car lit up the side of the house. There were a few other cars parked along the road. Beyond the house I could see the dark shapes of people standing together in the field. I could hear them talking and laughing. From somewhere came the faint tinny jangle of music from a radio.

I walked out toward where they were gathered. David and Angeline were there in the twilight with a dozen other men and women. They had a cider press set up in the grass. Mounded in woven baskets, apples gleamed red and gold in the light of the porch lamps. David was kneeling down turning the hand crank of the press and they were dumping apples into the grinder. The fresh juice, fragrant and deep amber, dripped through a spout into a steel pail on the ground. Everyone had a cup and occasionally someone would hold theirs under the spout and let it fill with the trickling juice.

It was still two weeks before the first frost and the women were in thin sweaters and their husbands stood in jackets or shirtsleeves in the mild evening. The radio was playing music in the house and it was turned up so we could just hear it outside. Angeline came over and pressed my hand. She was starting to show. There was a softness to her body that I had not noticed before. Under her dress and sweater a slight mound to her belly. She was smiling. Her hair and eyes shone in the lamplight and her cheeks were flushed from laughter. She was very lovely.

I drank apple juice out of an enameled metal cup and it was sweet and had a warm tang. After a while I wanted a whiskey and soda and I left the party and went up into the house. I walked back into the kitchen to look for a bottle of soda in the pantry. They had been canning vegetables and there were cardboard boxes of empty mason jars stacked on the floor against the wall. Large deep pots still stood on the stove where they were boiling the jars. Sealed jars of tomatoes, green beans, and corn in brine stood in rows on the table waiting to be taken down to the cellar. Angeline appeared in the doorway. She smiled and came over and took my hand.

"Come with me, Father," she said. "I want to show you something."

She led me upstairs and down a darkened hall into a part of the house I didn't know well. We stopped at the door of a room and she went inside to turn on a lamp. I waited at the doorway. She found the lamp and in the warm light I saw that the room had been made into a nursery. Everything was white and pale blue. A rocking crib sat waiting in the corner. She looked at me and smiled. I could tell how happy she was.

"Sarah and I have been working on it," she said.

"It's beautiful."

"I just wanted you to see it. You've been such a good friend to us."

"If there's ever anything you need, I want you to come and tell me."

"I will," she said.

We went back downstairs and I stepped into the kitchen. I found a fresh bottle of soda in the pantry.

Sarah came in and we stood at the counter talking for a few minutes before she disappeared into the cellar looking for something for the party. I was left alone in the empty kitchen. I could hear the voices outside and the radio in the parlor. There was a sound inside the front door and I looked down the hallway. It was dark but the light from the porch was shining through the screen door, gleaming on the polished wood floor.

Inside the door two shadows leaned together in the hall. I watched them. David and Angeline stood in silhouette against the lamplight shining through the door. He was talking to her in a low voice, leaning close to her ear with her hand clasped in his resting over her belly. She turned her face up and gave him a lingering kiss. Then he opened the door and they went out together.

I waited and then followed them outside. For hours we all stood in the field drinking cider and talking. As it got later people gradually started to say goodbye and go home. We listened to the sad, pacifying sound of the cars pulling away in the gravel. By moonrise it was just us three. We laughed and told stories a long time until the conversation faded, and we just sat quietly on the steps enjoying the night.

The only sounds were the wind moving the tops of the trees and the faint voice of the radio from inside the house. At midnight we sat under the trellis in the stars and wild grapes. The moon was almost full. The air was cool and crisp, and in the dark we could smell the dusky sweetness of the ripening scuppernongs. The moon lingered low over the shadow of the hills and fell. For the first time it started turning cold in the night.

27

At dawn I came out on the porch and waited. The late November sun glinted over the mountains in the east. I watched it rise bright and cold, squinting in the cold light. In the bottom of the basin the river lay in the last remnant of night and the horizontal light cut across the valley, casting a line of shadow along the buildings. The top of the church stood there illuminated, cold and white against the steel-colored sky. My breath steamed in the clear morning air, my eyes watered. The brilliant cold almost hurt.

Somewhere down the road I heard the truck coming. A moment later it appeared along the tracks, the glass and chrome flashing coldly through the trees. I stood and walked a few steps out into the yard and waved. The truck pulled along the fence and stopped with the scrape of tires in the gravel, the deep murmur of the idling engine and the smell of gasoline in the morning air. Gray smoke leaked out of the exhaust. There were two men in the cab and three others in the back. Bo and another man jumped down out of the bed and came up into the yard.

"What say there, Father."

"Hey boys."

"Cold enough for you?"

"Just about."

"You ready?"

"I am. How about a hand up here—"

They followed me up onto the porch. I had two crates filled up and ready. They looked at all of it.

"You're not going to need all this," Bo said.

He crouched and started rummaging through the crates, first one then the other. He pulled out the bedroll and canteen and handed them to me.

"We brought a rifle and shells for you. Do you have a knife?"

"It's there—"

He found the knife in its sheath and handed it to me.

"You won't need the rest," he said.

"All right."

I opened the front door and they set the crates inside. They walked back toward the truck and I shut the door and stuffed the loose gear into my duffel and followed them. They reached down and pulled me up in the bed after them. The truck shifted in gear and turned out into the road, slowly at first and then with more speed until the noise of the wind and the engine buried everything. I watched the rectory and the church grow small behind us and finally disappear behind the trees.

The truck flew along in the crisp November air. I pulled my cap down around my ears. Even in the sharp cold I enjoyed the open sky and the wind. When I wanted to say something even to someone sitting right there, I had to yell right into his ear and he'd grin and nod with the wind blowing all over the place, even if he hadn't clearly heard what I'd said.

We pointed and smiled at things we saw on the road, things up on the mountainside or down in the bottom along the river.

The sun climbed in the morning sky and started to warm the world, burning off the last morning haze. We followed the river on the thin ribbon of asphalt that ran along the valley's edge. In the early afternoon we turned up a dirt road that climbed and curved around the side of a steep mountain slope. The truck pitched and shuddered in the ruts. We held the gear down in the bed with one hand and clung to the walls with the other. The chassis slammed into a hole and the boys in the cab turned and grinned back at us when we hollered to take it easy.

Finally the truck slowed as the road faded into a rocky track and became a path littered with dry dead stumps and fallen tree trunks. We pulled up and stopped in the pine needles along the trees. The engine died and we stood up and stretched and looked out into the valley. The mountains stretched out, mottled rocky brown and deep green with pine woods, the sky blue and flat and endless above them. The boys jumped down out of the truck and we started handing the crates down over the open back gate.

By the time we'd set up camp it was late afternoon. The sun had lost its heat and slanted coldly through the pines. The boys were tying their tent flaps down and starting to split up and disappear into the trees with their rifles. Everyone took off away from the camp in a different direction. Bo came out of the tent with a rifle in each hand and looked at me.

"Father?"

"I'm ready."

"All right then," he said. "Let's go."

We started down a ridge that ran a distance and then flattened out into a silent pine forest. His breath bloomed palely in the air ahead as I trailed him. We walked in the quiet with our rifles slanting across our chests. We spotted a few men waiting in makeshift blinds, spying for animals coming up to feed or rut. Some perched in the crooks of trees, some hidden in thickets. They crouched mute and still in the brush, acknowledging us with only a glance as we passed.

Dusk fell clear and cold behind the trees. A pale blue sky swept by glaucous clouds. We came up over a ridge into a stand of cedar and pine. Beyond, a sloping meadow opened in the trees, the dark rim of mountains running the horizon. Bo stopped and studied the bark of a few close-growing saplings. He nodded to himself. Kneeling, he took up handfuls of dirt and pine needles and rubbed them over his gloved hands and overalls to kill his scent. He glanced at me and I followed suit. We went on.

The air was cold and still when we reached the verge of the trees.

"All right," he said. "This here'll do."

We ducked and crawled up under a pine bower, crouching in the low shadowed chamber it formed. Dense boughs concealed us on either side. In front of us a clear view of the ridge and the glade. Bo knelt, resting the rifle over his knee and peering out into the field.

For what seemed like a long time we crouched there mutely gripping our rifles. The setting sun glinted palely through the pine boughs. Across the glade the trees swayed faintly in the wind. Shadows lengthened across the field, joining and deepening in the dusk. The sky was clear and cold in the falling light. Bo bit from a tobacco plug and would turn his head and spit brown juice down into the dry pine needles. We waited in the silence, looking out over the blue meadow.

At first they were just shadows. I couldn't tell if it was only the wind moving the branches. Then they started coming up silently out of the trees into the clearing. There were three of them. I could see others lingering back along the tree line. They hesitated, tasting the air as they came. I looked over at Bo. He was already squinting down the barrel of his rifle.

The deer came up into the meadow and stopped, lifting their heads. They could smell us. Bo took aim on a magnificent antlered buck. It loomed there so awesome that it seemed immortal, impossible to kill. He held the rifle perfectly still. The world seemed to stop and tremble as he drew sight on the beast. Beyond the field the sun glinted red and died along the horizon. The animals stood motionless in silhouette. The sky turned to gold behind them. The great buck froze, straining its senses, aware that it was being hunted.

I watched the drama from a tangle of briars. I held my breath. My heart was pounding in my chest. My rifle lay useless in the pine needles.

Sometimes, all of a sudden, a clarity and a silence come and hush over everything. Every stone and every leaf stands forward and confesses its true self and its perfection. Everyone you know is saintly and true, and all their sins become steps on a path to some final glory. There is no future or past: all the doors stand wide open and always have, and the world breaks your heart and saves you at the same moment with its truth.

He fired once and the shot rang out breaking the silence of the glade. The animals scattered and vanished back into the woods. The buck collapsed, shot dead where it stood, a dark, star-shaped wound just behind the eye.

The carcasses of half a dozen deer hung upside down in the cold November afternoon. Their back hooves were tied with lengths of rope to a raw wooden beam under the eaves of the shed. Their throats had been cut and their heads hung loose, eyes glazed over, the dark blood dripping thick into the earth.

A hunter cut the throat of the last animal with a heavy curving knife. The blood steamed in the dust. He reached and cut down an enormous buck that had already been bled out. It fell heavily to the ground and he took it and hauled it out from under the shed.

He laid it out across a crude pine bench stained dark with blood like some rustic altar. The eyes staring up dark and still as carved wood. The tongue jutting over pale bloodstained teeth aslant in the gaping mouth. Blood crusted in the black nostrils and dripped coldly, pooling viscous and dark in the cold ground. The blade slid under the taut hide and began to tear away the skin.

28

In the late afternoon I heard the last confession. I lingered a few moments while the girl left the booth, waiting until she had gone. I sat in the cool shadowed space and closed my eyes, smelling the polished wood and old leather upholstery, the dust and the clean youthful smell of the child who had been there a moment before.

I took a deep breath and opened my eyes and stepped out into the room. The air was cool and dry, carrying the faded taste of incense and candle wax. The late November light leaned in through the high windows. A few candles burned down in the darkened nave. The church was empty now, except for a solitary old woman kneeling in front of the iron candelabra at the altar rail.

The big door opened and the pale afternoon light stretched in along the aisle. I thought that it must be the child returning for some reason, but when I looked I saw that it was Angeline. She wore a long coat but I could see the outline of her abdomen underneath. Her dark hair long and straight at her shoulders like a young girl. She was pale and beautiful. She came toward me and I smiled and took her hand.

"Hello, Father."

"Angeline, is this a business call?"

"No."

"I'm up at your house just about every week. You should be calling me Nathan by now."

"All right," she said. "I'll try."

"It's always good to see you. You don't need a reason to come down here."

"I know that. Thank you. This time I have one though."

"All right."

"I came to ask you for help."

"Whatever I can do—"

"I'm worried about Daniel."

I looked at her. Her face was shining. I could tell she had been crying. I took her arm and we went around to the outer aisle and sat down in the back along the last bench.

"What happened?"

"I don't know," she said. "Nothing. Two months ago I went out to see him at his place. I tried to give him a little money. He said he didn't want my help and not to come see him anymore. I told David about it and he made me promise I wouldn't go up there again."

"What do you want me to do?"

"Could you go up there and see if he's all right? I'm worried about him. That he's drinking. He could get sick. He could die up there by himself and nobody would even know about it. There's nobody up there to take care of him."

"I don't believe I've seen him at Mass since at least March," I said. "Even when he did come, it was never on a regular basis. I never did get to know him too well."

"Nathan—"

"Yes?"

"If my husband knew I was asking you to do this he might be upset."

I leaned forward and pressed her hand.

"It's all right," I said. "He won't have to know about it."

I pulled the car over on the shoulder of the hilltop and shut off the engine. There was still plenty of light. I set the brake and left the car on the side of the road and started walking up the path.

The hollow stretched back into the side of the mountain, a wide cleft with a creek running in the bottom. The path ran up from the road along a ridge. As I climbed I could see the ribbon of dark water, on its surface the reflected sheen of sunlight filtering through the trees. The woods were all brown now and pale gold, and up on the higher slopes the deep shadows of evergreens.

The air felt mild along the hollow and had the cool taste of the stream and damp earth and decaying leaves. The water whispered quietly in the bottom and everything was still and lovely. It felt good walking along the mountainside. I let myself follow the climbing path without thought, enjoying the exercise. I loved the subdued reds and golds on the trees and the living hush of the woods.

The trail came up on a level that was like a small plateau on the shoulder of the mountain where the hollow opened up and shallowed and spread out into an alley of clustered cedar and pine. I stopped and looked. The path faded there and seemed to split off in two directions. I turned to the right and walked down into the trees.

By the time I realized I'd gone the wrong way, the sun had fallen behind the mountain and the shadows were lengthening into dusk. I stopped and looked ahead through the trees. In the twilight I could see the line of the path veer down the slope, running along the far side of the hollow and down toward the road. I turned and started back to where the trail had split.

As it grew darker the path became less clear. My feet crunched in the layer of dead leaves on the ground. Gradually the sagging branches became just shadows against the dark gray of the undergrowth. I heard the whisper of running water somewhere off in the dark. The air took on a cool dank taste. Night fell as I walked. Over my head the dry autumn boughs became a black canopy.

Ahead of me the path opened up into a glade. Through the gap in the trees the stars shone cold and white in the stillness of the night sky. There was no moon. I could see the cabin, small and gray against the darker woods. A thin line of smoke rose straight up from a pipe in the roof and dissolved in shadow. A feeble light shone pale in one window.

I walked up the path and stopped under the trees at the edge of the clearing. I stood and listened. The shack was still in the silence of the glade. I could see the smooth worn dirt path running through the grass up to the porch.

I moved forward into the clearing and then stopped and stood still. In the window a shadow moved across the light. There was a noise like the crash of breaking glass and then the creak and snap of splintering wood. Then I could hear a voice.

It started low. Husky and guttural in the silence. It spoke but the words slurred like the end of a long drunk.

I listened out in the dark. I didn't make a move.

Gradually the voice grew wild and violent, climbing to a shrill pitch. It erupted in curses and screams. It seemed to threaten and blame. I strained to make out its twisted language. I stayed still where I was, out in the dark crouched down along the trees, transfixed. The hair stood up on the back of my neck.

I waited out in the night and listened to him rage. The noise was otherworldly, insane. I stayed there frozen with my eyes closed. My heart pounded in my chest. Again came the sound of shattering glass and the voice grew more brutal, more senseless until it finally broke down into hoarse choking sobs.

I stood and listened until it became a faint ragged wail like the keening of a tortured dog. I felt sick to my stomach. For a long time I kept still. Then I turned silently and made my way back along the path in the dark.

The next day I went up to see her in the afternoon. David was still at work. The sky was clear and pale blue and I drove up slowly through town. I passed by children walking home from school with their books and they waved as I drove on. At the edge of town beyond the tracks the house stood white against the auburn woods. Along the treetops dry vestiges of leaves turned in the wind.

I pulled into the drive and parked and came up the walk. Out in the field the leaves had been raked into mounds of gold, orange, and brown. The garden was bare, with only the dry stubble of cornstalks. The withered remnants of vines hung on the arbor. Somehow in the air hung the vague sense of memory and longing that always comes with autumn. I went up on the porch and knocked and looked in the glass.

After a few moments Angeline came up the hall. She had on an apron over her big stomach and she was wiping her hands on the cloth. She looked through the glass and saw me and managed a smile. She opened the door and kissed my cheek and told me to come in.

Standing there with one hand still twisted in the damp fabric of the apron, she looked at me as if she might divine something in my face. She must have seen some hint there.

"Is everything all right?"

"I went up there," I said.

"Did you talk to him?"

"He was there, but I didn't see him—"

"What happened?"

"I should've gotten up there in the light of day," I said. "I got lost somehow up there in the woods. It was dark by the time I found his place. I saw a light and chimney smoke, but I didn't go up to the house. I was afraid he might think someone was up there to bother him—"

"Is he all right?"

"I think so. I'm not sure."

For a moment she studied my face.

"What happened up there, Nathan?"

"Nothing," I said.

I reached out and touched her shoulder. I tried to smile.

"He's going to be all right," I said. "Right now I think he needs us to pray for him."

29

In December the world turned bleak. Everything on the mountains looked desolate and drab. The river dropped in its bed, filthy and gray. The days were winding down, brief and stark, the light tired and dilute. Trees leaned dark and austere in the wind. Dirty snow limned the tracks. In town children bowed their heads in the frozen rain on their way to school. Morning frost rimed the windows of shops and in the afternoon icicles dripped under the eaves in the cold dead light.

I pulled the car up along the curb and parked on the street. I climbed the entrance steps in the dirty slush. The lobby of the hospital was silent and cold. A clerk looked up as I passed the desk. I came up the stairwell and through the open doors into the upper hall. No one was at the desk where the ward nurse usually sat. The morning light shone gray on the pale walls and everything was still.

I could hear voices speaking low and faint in some other room. I went down the ward along the beds. The screen had been removed and I saw that his bed was empty. The sheets and all the linens had been stripped, exposing the bare mattress. I stood at the side of the bed. The books and letters were gone from the bedside table.

I looked back. A nurse was coming down the ward. She saw me and came over.

"I'm very sorry," she said. "He passed away last night."

I didn't say anything.

"Are you all right, Father?"

"I went hunting," I said. "I never got to tell him that."

She looked at me. She didn't understand.

"Father, you knew he was in a lot of pain," she said. "Now he won't suffer anymore."

"I know. Thank you. I'm the one who should be comforting you."

We stood there for a moment without saying anything.

"Some of his things are here," she said finally. "Nobody has come to collect them. Can I give them to you, Father?"

"Yes," I said. "It's all right. I'll take them."

By February everything looked dead along the valley. I stopped the car along the side of the dirt path. It was drizzling in the muddy road. The rank smell of stale oil along the tracks. Across the field through the bare trees I could see the superintendent's house, stark and white in the rain.

I walked in the mud to the small gray cinderblock house. I went up through the soggy yard onto the porch and knocked. I waited but nobody came. I looked in the darkened window and knocked again. Someone moved inside.

After a moment Mary Beth opened the door. Her face looked awful. It was dark and swollen on one side. Her lip was split. She wouldn't look straight at me.

"I haven't seen you all at Mass in a while," I said. "I just wanted to stop by and make sure you were all right."

"I'm all right," she said. "I'm sorry Father, I got to go."

She was ready to close the door.

"What happened, Mary Beth?"

She looked down and shook her head without speaking.

"Is Ed here?"

"He's not here," she said. "I don't know where he is, Father."

Her voice caught in her throat and her face went to pieces.

"He run off last night and hadn't come home."

"Can I come in?"

"All right," she said.

She started to sob. She pushed the screen door open for me and we went back into the house.

In the night the wind had bent the trees, leaving them twisted and crusted in ice. With their bare dark bodies contorted they looked as if they were still cowering after some trauma. The warped branches glistened in the weak sunlight. In the clearing beyond, the shack dripped with melting ice. A plume of blue smoke leaked out of the roof pipe and faded into the bleak morning sky.

In the room a fire guttered in the stove. Daniel sat on the edge of the bed with his elbows on his knees. He got up and crossed the room and opened the drawer of the battered desk. Inside was the tarnished gray metal box. He looked at the box for a moment and then gently ran his fingers across its surface.

He opened it and inside was a pair of old blued steel revolvers. He pulled out one of the guns and held it, cradling it gently in his lap. His fingers moved over the heavy dark metal. For a few moments he sat on the edge of the cot looking straight ahead, the gun resting in his lap. Then he closed his eyes. He lifted the gun barrel and held it against his temple.

Bobby lit a cigarette. A distorted voice sang hillbilly out of a broken radio. He leaned behind the counter and smoked in the greasy light.

The door opened and Joe stood on the stoop under the porch lamp and stamped his boots. He stepped into the room and closed the door behind him. His overcoat glistened with ice and beaded water. Bobby looked over at him.

"Happy Valentine there, Joe. Your sweetheart aint in here."

"You're funny."

"Good to see you're alive," Bobby said. "Can I get you something?"

"I'm here aint I?"

"All right then."

Joe took off his coat and shook it by the door. The water dripped on the warped floorboards. He hung it on a peg along the wall and came over and sat on a stool at the counter. He peered through the smoke into the dark mirror behind the bar.

Bobby set the butt of his cigarette in the notch of a black iron ashtray on the bar. He leaned down under the counter and pulled a ceramic gallon jug out of a cupboard and poured clear liquid into a shot glass. He set the glass in front of Joe and stood back again and picked up his cigarette.

Joe drank the whiskey and asked for another and one more after that. When the drinks hit him he started feeling loose, leaning back in his seat and talking loud.

"Here's something I'd like to know," Bobby said. "What in the shitfire and damnation has got into your boss?"

"Meaning?"

"Meaning him marrying a woman and her husband hardly cold yet in the ground. And her already with child and set to deliver all in under a year—"

"I don't like it no more than anybody else," Joe said.

He tilted his head back and drained the shot glass. He set it on the wood empty and glanced up at Bobby and nodded wordlessly with the whiskey still burning in his throat. Bobby took it and poured another shot and set it up on the bar.

The door opened and a man came in out of the night. He was thin, nearly emaciated. He wore a thick beard, his coat ragged and dark, his dark hair hanging down the back of his stained cap. His black eyes and pale skin shone in the electric light. He glanced over at Joe sitting at the bar then lowered his eyes and looked away. His face fell under the shadow of his cap. He stepped up to the far end of the bar. He dug in his pocket and slid twelve bits onto the wood.

"I'd have two jars," he said in a flat voice without looking up.

Bobby glanced at him and looked back at Joe, ignoring the money on the bar.

"I aint saying one way or another," Bobby said. "I wasn't there. It's just that he married her it weren't three months past when they put him in the ground. Hell, I'd say closer to two."

Joe leaned back in his seat, already drunk. He looked at Bobby with disdain.

"Well, I was there," he said. "He picked that old boy out by name to go down in that hole. Two months later he marries his widow. What the hell do you think?"

Bobby leaned back against the counter and stared at Joe. He picked up his cigarette from the ashtray and looked absently away and smoked, shaking his head in disgust. For a long moment no one said anything. Finally the ragged young man standing in the shadow at the end of the bar spoke.

"How about them jars?"

His voice came flat and cold in the stillness of the room. Bobby turned and stared at him.

"Do I know you, mister?"

"For godsake don't give the man no trouble," Joe said. "Just let him have what he asked for. He aint the law."

Bobby looked askance at Joe.

"All right then," he said. "Just hold your horses."

He came out from behind the counter and stepped through the door into the back room. Joe sat gazing absently into the filthy mirror behind the bar, listening to the fuzz coming from the radio. He glanced once down at the pale man wrapped in his stained and ragged overcoat, standing silent at the end of the bar.

A minute later Bobby returned with two mason jars of clear liquid. He stepped back behind the bar and set the jars on the counter and collected the silver. The young man took the jars. Bobby leaned down to make change from a cigar box under the counter. When he stood up with the coins the man was already gone.

Out in the dark Daniel hurried along the road with the jars of corn whiskey in the crook of his arm. He crossed into the woods and along the path he started to run. One of the jars dropped in the dark and broke on a rock. The clear liquid spilled out among the shards of broken glass, running along the earth like a libation, slowly disappearing in the cold black ground.

30

In the morning people settled along the benches and the altar boy came down behind them in the aisle with the censer swaying on the chain. The murmur of their voices ran susurrant and low under the architecture of chords that rose from the organ. Beneath everything was the whisper of shoes sliding over the bare wood floor.

David and Angeline moved down the aisle behind the crowd. He took her coat and the curve of her domed abdomen showed big under her dress. She strained to sit with a steadying arm on the bench behind her. She was due any day. They sat down near the front on the aisle and I looked out and saw them leaning together whispering. The acolytes lit the last candles along the brass lamps and the iron candelabra, then came down and stood behind the rail.

I stepped out of the vestry into the vaulted apse and waited in the sanctuary. I stopped and closed my eyes. Somehow the sacred music moved me in a way that was rare, that I had almost forgotten. I was wholly present, without any thought of invocation or host, valediction or sacrament. I felt only the raw presence of the congregation: the warm aura of their bodies, the faintly bitter tang of their exhaled breath, and the drafts of cold air coming through the door when someone slipped in late and settled discreetly in the back along the last shadowed pew. The deep suspirant drone of the organ filled the church until the final note of music held legato for a long moment and ended.

There was a noise outside. It sounded like two men at a distance disagreeing in raised voices. I stopped for a moment and listened. Everyone in the church could hear them. After a moment the voices stopped. I tried to go on with the Mass. Suddenly they started again, much closer this time. They were shouting and I could tell they were coming nearer. Everyone in the church turned and looked back toward the doors.

A second later there was a cry and the door slammed open as if someone had kicked it in. Daniel stood there in the doorway against the pale square of daylight. He was breathing hard in his dark beard and grimy white long john shirt. The pale steam of his breath bloomed against the shadow of the back wall. Another man came in after him. The man grabbed at his arm and Daniel pushed him down through the open door. He stood panting in the shadow at the back of the aisle. Then he stepped forward into the light.

There was the hush of shock. Then a murmur passed through the congregation. Daniel glared around the room, scanning the faces along the pews. His beard glistened with liquor or spittle or both. He spotted David and Angeline near the front. She closed her eyes and leaned her head into her husband. He put his arms around her and pulled her against him.

When Daniel started to speak, I could tell he was drunk. He stood in the back of the church and shouted.

“What is all this? Yall aint foolin nobody—you hear me? I know what’s goin on—I been to church—don’t think I hadn’t!”

There was a silence. Nobody moved. He stepped forward along the aisle and stared down anyone who looked at him. People lowered their eyes and turned away. His voice was wild and ragged as he quoted:

Blessed be the name of God for ever and ever:
For wisdom and might are his—
He revealeth the deep and secret things:
He knoweth what is in the darkness—

He was still going when three men stood up in the aisle and started toward him. Before he could come any further they had him by the arms. He struggled, ranting as they dragged him toward the doors.

The congregation erupted like a courtroom after an outrageous verdict. They started pouring out of the benches after them. I watched helplessly from the pulpit. I looked at Angeline. She went to pieces and buried her face in her hands. David leaned over, shielding her with his arms around her body. I came down through the gate in the altar rail and followed the crowd out into the daylight.

Across the valley the blue rim of the mountains ran the horizon and the chalk-colored sky hung there behind it. They had him down in the yard, pinned spread-eagled with a man on each limb. They were pushing his face into the frost-hardened ground. He kept trying to lift his head up and they kept slamming it back against the frozen turf. His cheekbone and the pale skin of his temple were rubbed raw. They had jammed something into his mouth and I could hear the muffled sound of his voice straining under the gag, his labored breath huffing through his nostrils.

I looked up along the ridge. Through the bare trees I could see the patrol car coming down the dirt road. It crested the ridge trailing a haze of gray exhaust and pulled up along the edge of the churchyard. Two peace officers left the car doors open and came over to where they had him pinned on the frozen ground. He was still trying to move and I saw the men lean down hard on him with their knees in his back.

An officer pulled the filthy gag out of his mouth. They handcuffed his wrists behind his back, stood him up, and started walking him toward the car. He stumbled along with his head hanging, gasping and hacking. Their exhaled breaths were gray plumes in the cold morning air. They got him to the car and leaned him over the hood. One of the officers fished in the pockets of his trousers.

"Take a look at this," he said to the other cop.

He held a pistol up by his fingertips. The blued gunmetal dark and cold in the pale light. They finished frisking him, opened the door, and leaned him down into the back seat of the car. Daniel sat with his head bowed, his lungs still working. There was blood and dirt smeared across the side of his face. Blood dripped from his nose and mouth where they had beaten him, glistening red on the dark bristles of his beard like the bloodied muzzle of some animal.

He spoke without looking up.

"I wasn't going to hurt nobody," he said.

A patrol car waited in the driveway. Two sheriff's deputies came up on the porch and knocked and stood waiting in the cold. David came to the door and shook their hands. He stepped back into the house and let them in. They followed him into the parlor and he asked them to sit down. They sat without taking off their hats or long coats.

"They've got him up at the state hospital," the deputy said.

David looked at him. He didn't say anything. The deputy spoke again in a low voice.

"Now, we can just warn him and turn him loose," he said, "or we can have them hold him up there for observation. You just say what you want us to do."

David sighed and studied him for a moment. Then he nodded vaguely and turned away, staring off into the pale winter light glowing in the window.

Daniel stood up. He stepped to the door of the narrow cell. Drab light slanted through the high barred window in the wall behind him. He was sober now. He went back and sat down on the cot against the cinderblock wall. He got up again and paced the tiny room, measuring its space.

He leaned against the door with his face pressed against the wire grill and listened. Somewhere down the hall he could hear the faint shuffle of footsteps.

"Hey—"

His voice rang down the corridor. He waited. There was no answer.

"Hey somebody!"

He was quiet for a long moment, listening for any movement or response. He strained for an angle to look down the hall, but the wire-covered hole was too small. He gritted his teeth.

"Get your goddamn asses down here or I'm going to tear this place up!"

The sound of his voice broke down the dark vacant hall, echoing hard and violent until it died. Again there was silence. He closed his eyes and pressed his forehead against the door. Then he sat down on the cold floor.

An hour later he was still sitting on the floor, leaning against the other wall with his arm on the cot. Outside the sun had fallen behind the hills, the light fading on the gray walls of the cell. He started to hear sounds from somewhere out in the hall. He sat still, listening to the faint noises of the patients. The voices of lunatics echoed down the halls from different parts of the ward. In the distance he could hear one of the inmates barking like a dog.

The Greeks believed that the gods loved what's temporary in man—his futile, suffering nature. They themselves were beyond pain and permanent loss, but the fleeting beauty of human struggle pleased them, and the poets told their pleasure to the world.

PART IV

31

I stood on the porch and looked out across the darkened yard toward the church. The windows were dark and the doors were closed for the night. Everything was cold and still. I stepped back inside the house and shut the door. I turned off the porch light, went back into the bedroom and turned on the bedside lamp.

It was cold in the house and I went in the kitchen and lit the gas. I turned on the light, went to the cabinet and took down a bottle and a glass from the cupboard. I sat down at the kitchen table, poured a shot of whiskey into the glass and drank it. Then I got up and went to the icebox and came back with a bowl of ice. I put a few shards in the glass and poured bourbon over it.

I had a third drink and put the bottle back, left the glass in the sink, and turned out the kitchen light. I went in the bedroom and got undressed, hung my clothes on the back of the chair and put on a nightshirt. There was an empty pitcher on the washstand and I took it into the darkened kitchen and filled it with water from the tap.

I came back in the bedroom and poured water into the enameled metal basin. Outside in the night the wind came up, bending the bare trees against the house. I went to the window and pulled the curtains closed. I stood at the washstand, leaned down and splashed the cold water on my face.

The door swung open at the top of the stairs. Warm light shone down from the kitchen into the gloom of the cellar. A shadow moved into the illuminated doorway and hesitated there. There was no sound or movement in the lower room. The figure in the door came halfway down the stairs, stopped again and peered down into the dark.

Against the far wall a man leaned over a desk in the glow of a coal oil lamp. The boy came down the bare wooden stairs onto the dirt floor. He moved through the darker region between the swath of glow falling down the stairs and the thin nimbus of lamplight beyond. Without speaking he came and stood by the desk and waited.

Mr. Wilkinson glanced absently at the boy. He turned back to the desk, dipped the pen in the glass inkwell and scratched a line across a square of paper. The ink glistened black in the wan light. He laid the pen down on the desktop and the ink dripped and pooled viscous and dark on the worn grain of the wood. He folded the paper in half and in half again and held it out to the boy. The boy looked at him and then reached out and took the folded square of paper. He turned wordlessly and went back across the cellar and up the stairs.

The door closed over the golden light from the room above. Mr. Wilkinson looked back at the darkened stairs. He rose from the desk and stepped over to the cot against the wall. He knelt there and pulled out the bag on the earth floor underneath. He turned the hasp on the worn leather valise and opened the bag. From beneath a few pale shirts he uncovered the dark metal of a revolver and a ruddy, paper-sheathed bundle of dynamite.

Daniel lay still on the bed in the darkened cell with his arm draped over his forehead as if he were asleep. A narrow band of light fell through the bars in the window, half illuminating his face. His eyes shone with reflected light as he stared up at the blank wall and ceiling. Nobody had come to see him since they'd delivered him in handcuffs. He was thirsty and he wondered what time it was.

Outside the door vague sourceless noises washed down the barren corridor. He lay still on the cot and listened. He thought he could hear a faint erratic scratching. He held his breath and he could feel his heart beating in his chest. There was a muffled sound like someone pulling a metal bed frame over the bare floor in some other room. Sometimes it sounded like there was distant laughter. He couldn't be sure. Voices seemed to call and respond to each other in senseless conversations. His heart started to race. He turned over and closed his eyes and tried to sleep, but it was no use.

Somewhere distant he thought he could hear wheels turning. He opened his eyes and listened, staring blankly at the painted gray cinderblocks that made up the wall. All traces of other sounds had faded. Now he was sure what he heard. Someone was coming down the hall. He listened to the wheels and the knock of footsteps coming closer in the corridor. The sound stopped outside the cell. At the door came the jangle of keys on a ring.

Metal scraped on metal and the lock caught, a hollow echo out in the corridor. The door opened and the dim light coming through the cell window bled into the shadow of the hall. Two orderlies in white uniforms stepped into the moonlit doorway. Behind them in the hall another man waited by a steel gurney. Daniel raised himself up on the cot and looked at them.

32

Outside in the night a few dry flecks of icy snow started to fall, glittering cold and silvery, reflecting the light that glowed in the windows of the house. Angeline stood over the sink and looked out in the dark at the drifting specks, glinting metallic in the void. She thought it had grown too cold for a deep, white snow.

Her eyes focused on the pane of glass and she traced her own reflection in its dark surface. Behind the counter the arc of her belly showed under the apron hanging loose around her swollen body. She opened the spigot and ran hot water over the dishes. The basin started to fill and steam rose up on the cold glass of the windowpane, obscuring the night beyond.

Behind her at the kitchen table Sarah finished packing a box of empty jars and started down the cellar stairs. Angeline went back in the dining room to finish clearing the supper table. She stopped in the doorway and turned out the lamp. She stood and listened. She could hear faint music coming from the parlor. On the table the rest of the dishes shone in the indirect light from the kitchen.

She went around the table stacking the plates. When she moved to lift them she felt it. She twisted in pain and the plates slid out of her hands and hit the edge of the table, smashing in jagged white shards across the floor. She tried to speak but her voice was lost in her panting breath. The pain came again and made her breathe shallow and quick. Weakly she cried David's name.

The force of her voice dissipated along the hall. She could hear the music coming faint and muted from the parlor. She gasped, clutching her abdomen with one hand and grasping at the edge of the table with the other to hold herself up. Again she called her husband's name back into the silence of the darkened house.

The boy turned down a dirt alley and ran behind a row of darkened houses. He moved along the shadowed outskirts, through zones of cold light cast wan and lambent from distant night lamps. As he ran he left a steaming trail of pale breath dissolving in the dark behind him. His steps echoed in the cold silence. Packs of feral dogs roamed the deserted streets, their shadows stretched vast and exaggerated in the road like the grotesque profiles of preternatural beasts.

He ran toward a light burning coldly in the last row of houses. Hurrying, he climbed the back stoop of the last small house at the end of the alley. He stopped there, out of breath. Down through the bare trees he could feel the presence of the river off in the dark. He knocked furtively on the screen door. Dogs were barking somewhere down the road. The door opened and a woman stood there and looked at him. She stepped back into the room and let him in and closed the door behind him.

The boy stood in the kitchen watching her. She gestured with her head toward a doorway. He stepped through into a small dimly lit parlor. A wood stove burned in the corner. He could see the embers glowing red through the iron grate in the stove door. Beside the fire a man sat in a rocking chair. Under the glow of a lamp a radio played music turned down so low it was barely audible.

The man looked at him standing in the doorway. The boy came across the room and stood by the fire. He dug in his pocket and brought out the folded piece of paper and handed it to him. The man unfolded the note and studied it silently. Then he leaned forward in the chair and opened the door of the stove and dropped the slip of paper into the fire.

The two men stepped forward into the room. Daniel started to get up.

"What's all this? Hold on now—"

He tried to get up but they were already on him. They took hold of his arms and shoulders and forced him back down onto the cot. He started to kick against them but they had him good. He twisted his neck to bite one of them but the other man caught him by the hair and jerked his head back and held it. Daniel's breath seethed in his throat. The orderlies glanced back toward the doorway. The man in the hall pushed the gurney into the cell behind them and started doing something Daniel couldn't see. He strained to look past the men on top of him but one of them had his forearm across his neck.

The man stood over them beside the cot. He turned away from the window. His face was in shadow but the edge of his spectacles glinted in the light from the window. He held up a hypodermic needle vertical in the air and pressed the plunger with his thumb until a translucent drop glistened at the tip. Daniel saw the needle flash in the half-light. He twisted his body in great heaving spasms under the weight of the men but they held him fast. The doctor leaned over him and looked into his face. He whispered a gentle silencing hush as he pushed the spike deep into Daniel's flesh.

"Shhhhhh—"

Daniel felt the needle go in and shoot its fluid into the muscle. He gasped and his body relaxed under the two men holding him down. His jaw gaped slack against the hard forearm of the orderly and his eyes stared up, glassy and vacant in the dark.

33

David opened the door. The doctor waited there in the cold. David stepped back in the hall and the older man came inside and closed the door. He set his bag down and took off his heavy coat and hat and David hung them in the closet. The doctor looked at him. David's face shone pale and anxious in the light of the hall lamp.

"Something's wrong, Cy—"

"It's going to be all right," the doctor said. "Where is she?"

"She's upstairs."

"How long ago did it start?"

"Right before I called you."

"Good," the doctor said. "I want you to call the hospital and tell them we're on the way."

"All right."

"You don't need to worry. Everything's going to be fine."

"All right," he said. "Thank you, Cy."

There were sounds coming from the upstairs. The two men stood there and listened. Sarah's voice was hardly audible, speaking in low soothing tones. The words she was saying were not clear. Then there were other, inarticulate sounds. There was a noise like a violent sighing breath that came in erratic gasps. Then came an incoherent, bestial whine. It died away into choking sobs. David looked at him. The doctor picked up his bag and started up the stairs and David followed him.

I sat up in bed for an hour reading. Finally I closed the book and set it on the bedside table and put down my glasses. I turned out the lamp and lay back and closed my eyes. I lay there a long time looking through a sliver in the curtains at the subtle glow from the night sky. I couldn't sleep. Without turning on the lamp, I got up and went to the closet and put on my trousers and jacket. I went out to the front room in the dark and slipped on a pair of shoes by the door. Then I stepped out into the night.

It had gotten even colder. I looked out across the field. The church loomed there featureless in the dark. The sky spread out above the clearing like a black canopy draped between the blacker shadows of the compassing woods. A great dark gap dusted with infinite glitter. Bejeweled, vast and lapidary with stars. For a long moment I stood outside the house gazing up at it in the cold. Then I started walking out toward the deserted church.

The headlights of the truck flashed through the bare black shapes of trees along the road ahead. A crust of rime ice still clung to the boughs, glittering cold and stark in the sweeping light. In the open bed of the truck, shapes of men sat huddled forward behind the darkened cab. The truck slowed around the last bend and started to climb. Cold gravel popped under the tires. Up at the top of the ridge the guardhouse lamp shone along the road. As the truck advanced, the pine-board shack took shape out of the dark. The plank of the lowered draw gate blocked the road beyond.

The truck pulled up along the berm of the road, its headlights illuminating the trees, throwing slanting shadows that wheeled in the light. The shadow of the narrow booth fell back in the road. The truck rolled to a stop with its lights shining on the door of the shack. The driver stepped out with the engine still running and left the door open behind him. He drew a pistol out of his coat, came around, and stood in front of the truck. Three men stood up in the truck bed. The barrels of their shotguns glinted cold and blue. They jumped down onto the road and spread out facing the shack.

The narrow door opened and two night guards stepped out into the headlights carrying shotguns. They blinked in the glare and tried to shade their eyes with their hands. They saw the silhouettes of the men and the shotguns leveled on them. The truck engine rumbled idle. Pale smoke leaked along the road in the dark. The driver spoke.

"Drop them weapons," he said.

The guards hesitated, watching him.

"Do it or you won't live to guard nothin else."

The two guards moved slowly, leaning forward slightly as they let their shotguns fall to the ground.

"Step out real slow past them shotguns."

The men obeyed. They took several steps out into the road. Their faces looked old in the harsh light. Their shadows leaned against the gray boards of the shack behind them.

"Now kneel down."

The two men knelt in the gravel, their eyes cast down in the glare. Their breath smoked opaque in the headlights. The driver turned and looked back into the darkened windshield of the truck. The passenger door swung open. Mr. Wilkinson stepped out of the cab. He came around the door and stood by the right headlamp and looked at the men kneeling on the ground. He stood there over the men for a moment, regarding them vaguely. The other gunmen watched him, their weapons trained on the kneeling guards. Finally Mr. Wilkinson turned and gave them a nod.

One of the guards looked up.

"Wait a second, don't—"

They raised the barrels of their shotguns and fired.

34

He was awake. He tried to move but couldn't. The doctor had already gone out of the cell and the two orderlies lifted him up off the cot and laid him on the gurney. They pulled the straps over him and fastened them loosely around his body and wheeled him out through the doorway into the darkened corridor. They moved along the hall in silence, the only sounds the echoing steps of the men and the rasp of the stretcher wheels. They passed through thin bands of light and he could see their faces flash above him for an instant before they entered the next expanse of shadow. They traveled for what seemed like a long time. Everything along the hall had the same dim gray look.

Finally they stopped at an open doorway. A pale light shone inside. They turned the stretcher and brought him through the door. In the middle of the room there was a table like a bed upholstered with dark leather. Metal buckles hung down from straps along the edge. They wheeled him along the far wall and stopped alongside a countertop. There was a metal basin and faucet set into the surface. The steel fixtures gleamed faintly in the light from across the room. The orderlies turned wordlessly and left him there.

For what seemed like a long time he lay there listening to vague sounds in the hall. He wasn't sure for how long. After maybe an hour had gone by a woman came in. She went to the other side of the room and stood by the lamp on the opposite counter. Her pen scratched against a clipboard. She raised her head and looked across the room. She started to come toward him. The light fell across her back. He couldn't make out her face.

She stood over the gurney. She had on a white dress. She turned in profile against the light and he saw her face. Her skin was pale and luminous. She put her fingers on his wrist and felt his pulse. She saw him looking up at her and she touched his hand and smiled down at him. She was beautiful. She went around to the counter and reached up and opened the cabinet above the sink. Light shone dully on the surfaces of steel vessels inside. She took down a bowl and closed the cabinet. She took a dry sponge out of a drawer under the counter.

From one of the drawers she produced a pair of electric clippers. In the wall along the top of the counter were power outlets and she plugged the cord into the outlet and turned a switch on the shears. They buzzed with a low mechanical hum. She rested her left hand on his forehead and started to shave his face. She moved the clippers over his jaw with gentle pressure. He could feel the whiskers falling away from his skin in dense clumps.

He could feel everything: the vibration of the blades on his face, the cold metal surface of the shears as they grazed him, the smooth cool skin of her hand resting gentle and firm on his temple, steadying him on the stretcher. She finished shaving his face and started to run the blades up onto his skull. His long hair fell away in thick dark locks. He could feel the cool air of the room and her hand moving over the bristles of his shorn scalp.

When she finished she laid the clippers on the counter. She set the basin down in the sink and turned on the water. Steam rose up in the bowl and clouded the steel. She was only a shadow standing over him but sometimes she turned in the light and he saw again how lovely she was. She moved the damp sponge over his skin gently, almost tenderly. She washed his forehead and temples without speaking, occasionally caressing his bare skull.

He was calm, passive, breathing steadily through his nose. He felt everything around him. It was all right. He lay still and watched the figure of the woman moving above him in the dim room.

David stood in the doorway and looked into the room. Dr. Perry was kneeling down at the side of the bed. His black leather bag was open on the floor beside him. Angeline was lying there with the covers thrown off. She had on a pale thin nightgown. Her skin was almost white. Her eyes were closed, her head leaning back against the headboard. Her face was drawn and exhausted. Sweat glistened on her skin in the light of the bedside lamp. The material of the nightgown was soaked through, clinging damply to her collarbones. Sarah was kneeling on the other side of the bed, leaning over and clasping her hand. She kept talking to her in a low voice. David could see where her hand was white from Angeline squeezing it.

Her knees were pulled up, a sheet draped over them. The cloth was wet and heavy with sweat and birth fluids, and pink with watery blood. The whole bed was soaked. A pungent smell hung in the room. Her nightgown was wet and clung to her pale limbs. Sarah washed the sweat from her face and the blood and birth fluids from her body. The doctor knelt by the bed listening with his stethoscope. He held her right wrist and looked at his pocket watch.

Dr. Perry got up and came out into the hall. He took David by the arm and brought him away from the door. They stood at the top of the stairs and leaned together. They could still hear Angeline's deep sighing breaths from inside the room. The doctor spoke to him in a low voice.

"She's set to deliver right now," he said. "We don't have the time to get her to the hospital. I want you to go in the other room and stay in there. You don't need to see this. You hear me? You stay in there no matter what you hear."

"What's wrong with her?"

The doctor looked down and shook his head.

"Sometimes these things can be tough," he said. "I've seen these before. Things aren't lined up right. The baby wants to come out but he can't. The mother just gets worn out from the pain of it."

"What can you do for her, Cy?"

"She's going to be all right. She's strong. It's just going to be a little rough on her."

David watched him. He took the doctor by the arm.

"I want you to save her," he said quietly. "No matter what you have to do. Even if it means losing the baby."

Dr. Perry looked at him for a moment. He didn't say anything.

A cry came from the bedroom that started low and rose until it was a shriek and dissolved into gasps. She wept pathetically and called his name. The doctor took David's arm and pushed him gently away from the door. He turned and went back into the bedroom and closed the door behind him. A moment later there was another cry, more desperate this time.

David shut his eyes and turned away from the door.

35

The truck moved down the hill from the guard post and pulled into the clearing. The whole camp stood still. The night sky deep black above the gap in the trees. A few dark shapes of clouds moved across the stars. The tires crunched in the cinders as the truck rolled up slowly and stopped. The engine died and the headlights went dark. For a moment the truck sat silent in the road.

The men in the back jumped down off the truck bed and came around toward the foreman's house. The passenger door opened and Mr. Wilkinson stepped out. He looked up at the buildings. The company house stood vacant and dark, a shadow against the night woods. A light winked on in the window of the small foreman's house next to the office.

The door of the house opened, leaking pale lamplight out into the road. Joe emerged wearing a long john shirt, pulling his suspenders up over his shoulders. He squinted out into the dark. After a moment his eyes adjusted to the faint light, and he made out the shapes of the men and the truck. He saw the dark lines of the shotguns slanting in their hands. He recognized their faces.

"What the hell is going on here?"

No one answered. The men leveled their shotguns on him without a word.

◆ ◆ ◆

I turned the key in the lock of the church and pushed one of the double doors inward. I stepped through and stood in the dark of the foyer. It was almost as cold inside as it was out in the night and my breath still came as steam. I closed the door behind me and looked down into the nave. It was pitch black. After a moment my eyes began to adjust. The windows appeared in rows along either wall, dim gray regions hanging in the blackness. The panels of stained glass even fainter, almost lost in the dark space of the empty church.

The dark polished wood of the pews shone in the dim starlight. The aisle was a black path dividing the room. I walked down toward the apse and stopped past the benches along the rail. There was no sound. Under the rail stood the wrought-iron candelabra studded with the pale stubs of extinguished candles. I knelt down on the padded bench. On the table was a box and I chose three candles out of it and set them in empty holes. I struck a match and lit them, inhaling the taste of burnt wax and phosphorus.

The light glinted on an image of the Virgin suspended above the candelabra. I looked up along the wall. The flickering play of the candle flames illuminated the stained glass panels, showing scenes of saints and martyrs suffering for God's glory and sinners punished for their transgressions. In the faint, wavering light I couldn't tell them apart. I bowed my head and prayed.

> *Our Father which art in heaven, Hallowed be thy name. Thy kingdom come. Thy will be done in earth, as it is in heaven. Give us this day our daily bread. And forgive us our debts, as we forgive our debtors. And lead us not into temptation, but deliver us from evil: For thine is the kingdom, and the power, and the glory, for ever. Amen.*

He was alone in the room. The nurse had gone out and he lay there waiting. Everything was in shadow. Lamplight from the far corner shone dully on the polished steel fixtures in the sink beside him. He looked up. Rows of extinguished lights lined the darkened ceiling. In the center of the room stood the leather-upholstered table. Hanging down from its sides were straps tipped with metal buckles. Muted footsteps shuffled somewhere down the hall.

The nurse came back into the room. She stood over the gurney and looked at him. Her face was benevolent and calm. Again she felt his pulse. She went to the upholstered table and starting doing something with her back turned to him. He could hear the rattle of the buckles on the ends of the leather straps.

A doctor came in from the hallway and said something to her. He stood over the gurney and looked down at him. His face shone pale and bland in the half-light. He leaned down over the stretcher and spoke in a mild voice.

"Are we ready?"

Two of the men stood in the middle of the room with their shotguns on Joe while the other two tied him to the chair. A naked bulb on a wire cast a harsh circle of light. Joe stared up at them hatefully but said nothing. The man kneeling by the chair finished tying his legs and stood. He produced the filthy rag of a handkerchief and pushed it in Joe's face. Joe looked at the sooty cloth and glared up at the man.

One of the gunmen stepped forward and put the barrel of his shotgun to his head. Joe slowly opened his mouth and the man pushed the rag inside. He labored to breathe out of his nose. The other man pushed the muzzle of the shotgun into the cloth and with the gun barrel jammed it further down Joe's throat. He gagged and winced as the man forced it in.

The men finished binding his hands behind the chair and stepped away and stood out at the edge of the light watching him. Joe sat there with the wet tip of the coal-stained rag spilling out of his mouth. His chest worked and his eyes rolled around the room. The gray shadow of whisker stubble showed on his jaw and throat in the harsh light. The thought crossed his mind that they might turn around and walk out and leave him like that.

On the dark perimeter of the room he saw a figure move. Mr. Wilkinson stepped forward into the light. He stood silhouetted in the glare, looking at Joe. He turned his head and the hard white light gleamed on his spectacles, illuminating the blank surface of his face. The other men waited.

For a long moment Mr. Wilkinson calmly regarded Joe. Then he spoke in a low flinty voice.

"I guess you might want to know why I'm here," he said. "What all this is about."

He reached in the pocket of his overcoat and produced a pair of dark calfskin gloves. Joe followed his movements, his eyes rolling like a trapped animal.

"Rights," he said. "Progress. A fair deal—"

Mr. Wilkinson nodded to himself and looked down as if in reflection as he put on the gloves. For a moment his hat shadowed the pale skin of his face. He glanced back at Joe.

"Those things are coming," he said absently. "They're coming."

Then his voice turned cold.

"But I am not a negotiator," he said. "You buried forty men up here for a few tons of coal. I'm here to punish you for what you done."

36

Angeline panted and arched her back, burying her face deeper into the soaking wet pillows behind her head. She shut her eyes tight and bit into the damp fabric, deadening the faint whine that escaped her lungs. Sarah was kneeling on the bed, leaning over her, holding her down by the shoulders, working to keep her still. Angeline's white arms entwined around Sarah's, her hands grasping at the sleeves of the older woman's dress. Her grip tightened and became frantic and then relaxed as the spasm passed through her body. Sarah leaned down and whispered to her.

"Shhhhh—it's all right honey—it's going to be all right—it's going to be fine now—just a little bit more—"

The pain came again and Angeline screamed, almost weeping. She gasped and caught her breath and her words came plaintive and choked, her voice sounding distant and faint.

"Make it stop," she said. "Make it stop—"

Her words broke off into sobs. Sarah looked at the doctor.

"Isn't there something you can give her?"

He hesitated a moment and then nodded. He leaned down and picked up his bag and set it on the bedside table. He opened it and took out a hypodermic needle and a vial of clear liquid. He pierced the foil membrane and held it upside down in the light and pulled back the plunger of the syringe and watched it fill with the drug.

Sarah held her still and he pushed the needle into the pale wet flesh of her arm. In a moment Angeline's grip eased and she sank back into the bed, breathing slowly.

Dr. Perry pulled the sheet away and examined her again.

"It's tearing her up," he said. "I'm going to have to cut her to get it out."

He went in his bag and handed Sarah an opaque glass bottle and a wad of clean white gauze.

"Get ready to cauterize," he said.

He took out several scalpels and laid them in gauze on the table. The instruments gleamed in the light. He took out a bottle of alcohol and poured it over the knives. The smell of it permeated the room. He took out a short piece of leather and gave it to Sarah and told her to put it in Angeline's mouth and hold it there.

She was sobbing and the bit muffled the sound so that it was only a low whimper coming through her nose. The sheet was soaked through with birth fluid and blood. The doctor pulled it aside, heavy and wet. He took one of the knives from the table. Angeline opened her eyes and gasped. Her body tensed and jerked and through the gag she cried out with the pain of being cut open.

The doctor stood by the table and watched the orderlies strap Daniel down. He had on wire rimmed eyeglasses and he was bald and wearing a white coat with his stethoscope hanging around his neck. He was holding a clipboard.

They had turned on the light and it hung above the table in a metal shade. Daniel blinked in the glare. The orderlies finished buckling the straps across his body and the doctor told them to step back from the table. He came over and held Daniel's wrist and looked at his watch. He wrote on the clipboard and stepped back behind the table and started doing something Daniel couldn't see.

The nurse stood behind Daniel and steadied his head with her hand. In her other hand she had a wooden tongue depressor and she used it to daub something like vaseline on his temples. It felt cool against his skin. He could smell its bland, rancid odor. He tilted his head and looked back at her upside down. In the harsh light she did not look beautiful anymore.

She reached down to his face and told him to open his mouth. He felt something cool and smooth against his tongue. She closed his mouth over it and he bit down into the rubber. His breath came slow and even through his nostrils. He looked up at the faces of the orderlies standing back from the table. They had on blank expressions and seemed to stare ahead at nothing.

He heard a click and a low hum from behind and they were putting something against his temples where the vaseline was. There was a jolt and he heard a buzzing and then a roaring noise and a brilliant light exploded behind his eyes and he felt a heat and electric fire and his body jerked and contorted on the table and his heart exploded and his chest worked like a bellows and there was a singed smell in his nostrils. They shut it off but his muscles kept wanting to grip and seize. The room started to spin. They threw the switch again and his body jumped and poured sweat, the veins popped out of his forehead and he strained every muscle to the breaking point against the leather straps that held him down.

Mr. Wilkinson stepped forward and slammed his gloved fist into Joe's face. In the silence the punch struck with a dull, sickening smack. Blood and spittle ran out of the old man's nose and mouth and down his chin and his head sagged. Tears were streaming down his cheeks. The rag in his mouth dripped heavy and wet. His whole body slumped forward against the ropes. Ed Summers took a handful of his thinning hair and jerked his neck back. His ruined face shone pale and bloodied under the electric light.

"All right," Mr. Wilkinson said. "Hold him still there."

Two of the miners stood behind the chair and pulled Joe upright. Blood and snot thickened in his nostrils and the old man choked against the blood-soaked gag. They forced his head back all the way. Under the light the whites of his eyes glistened dully.

Mr. Wilkinson walked over to the stove in the corner of the room. The coals had burned down to ruddy embers glowing in the bottom. He stood there and took off his gloves and put them back in his coat. He crouched down and stretched out his hands in the heat of the stove. Out of the corner of his eye Joe watched him. For a moment Mr. Wilkinson closed his eyes and flexed his hands in front of the fire, extending his fingers and bringing them back into clenched fists.

Finally he opened his eyes and glanced back at Joe. Without saying anything he reached over and picked up a pail of coal dust sitting at the foot of the stove. He stood up and moved to the edge of the light carrying the blackened pail.

He nodded to Ed Summers. Ed leaned down and pulled the bloody rag out of Joe's mouth. Joe panted and hacked and the blood and phlegm dripped down his chin. The other man pulled Joe's head back again. From inside his coat Ed Summers took out an oil-stained length of steel chain. The grimy metal links clattered dully.

Joe twisted his neck to look back but the chain was already around his head. He felt the grease and cold weight of it sliding over his mouth and the tightening pull forcing his neck back. The steel links slid in the blood that still seeped out of his nostrils and swollen cuts. He could hear the men curse him as they worked the chain into his mouth like a horse bit.

They held him upright with their knees against the back of the chair as they pried open his jaw. The blood had begun to congeal in his nose and he labored to breathe. He tried to twist his head free and slip the chain but they had him good. An inhuman noise came up out of his throat like the lowing of a doomed animal. In the back of his mouth he could feel the metal grinding against his teeth. He tried to upend the chair but they caught him and held him straight and he slumped back again panting and choking on the bloodslicked chain.

Mr. Wilkinson stepped forward holding the pail. He stood over Joe, blocking out the light. He leaned and rested his knee on the chair seat and pushed it into Joe's groin. The men pulled hard on the chain, forcing his head back and his mouth open wide. Joe gagged and let out a pathetic, inhuman sound.

Mr. Wilkinson tilted the pail against his chin until the black dust and bits of crushed coal spilled into his mouth.

Joe's eyes opened wide. He twisted his body against the ropes as he gagged but they held him up straight in the chair. He writhed and choked on the grime. They let the chain fall out of his mouth and he pitched forward and hacked against the grit in his throat. The mire smeared and caked on his face like a mask, the wet black mud of bloody coal dust glistening under the light.

Mr. Wilkinson stood back and regarded him coldly. Joe was still leaning forward in the chair, spitting up blood and black phlegm, hacking to catch his breath. His eyes bulged in his head, the viscous black mix of blood and grit smeared on his face. Mr. Wilkinson reached in his coat and drew out his revolver. Joe looked up. He was frantic now, writhing against the ropes. Mr. Wilkinson looked at Ed Summers. He and the other man moved back away from the chair.

Mr. Wilkinson stepped calmly forward and pressed the pistol barrel against Joe's temple. Joe squinted his eyes shut and heaved against the ropes. The pistol made a flat dead pop. Joe slumped over, his limp body pulling against the ropes that still bound him to the chair.

The doctor stood up and wiped his hands on a fresh towel. He turned away from the bed and went into the bathroom and ran water in the sink. The water swirled pink in the basin as he scrubbed his forearms clean of the drying blood, dark and sticky to his elbows. He dried his hands and took off his glasses and rubbed his eyes. He stood and looked in the mirror for a moment, then shut his eyes and took a deep breath. He turned and stood in the doorway and looked back into the room.

Sarah knelt at the foot of the bed wringing a wet cloth over a basin on the floor. The room stank of sweat and the metallic reek of stale blood. The sheets were completely pulled away. Angeline lay motionless on the bed. Her dark hair had come loose and clung in damp strands to her pale face and neck. Sarah rinsed the cloth again and wrung it out. She sat on the edge of the bed and began to wipe Angeline's legs clean. Dr. Perry stepped back into the room. He went to the table and collected the instruments and closed the bag.

The baby lay on a towel spread out on the bed beside Angeline. It was ashen and silent and did not cry or move. The doctor watched it for a moment. Then he looked away. Sarah wrung the cloth dry and began to wipe its pale body clean of blood.

They were waiting in the truck with the lights off and the engine running. Ed Summers looked in the rearview mirror, back toward the company house. The windows were dark. There was no movement. He dug in his coat and lit a cigarette. The two other men crouched silent in the truck bed with shotguns leaning. The few flakes had stopped and the sky was vast and black over the clearing. The stars shone coldly on the hood of the truck, colorless in the dark. The whole camp stood dead still.

He looked back again and Mr. Wilkinson was coming off the front steps and into the gravel, walking fast. He had his bag in his hand and his spectacles glinted in the red glow of the taillights. Ed flicked his cigarette in the cinders and put the truck in gear. He watched Mr. Wilkinson in the rearview mirror. He came around and got in the truck and sat in the passenger seat, looking straight ahead.

"Let's go," he said.

Ed hit the gas and the truck spun in the gravel with a grinding scratch and they took off up the hill. Mr. Wilkinson stared straight ahead out along the road. Ed kept looking back over his shoulder at the camp.

There was a boom and the sound of shattering glass and he looked back. Black smoke was coming up against the trees and the small foreman's house was completely gone, the company house in flames. The truck came up the hill and onto the dirt road past the guardhouse and the dead men in the road. Ed looked back one last time and saw the company house burning out of control, the flames climbing in the night, roaring lurid and red against the black void of the sky.

37

The snow on the mountain shone in the early light, the trees bare and dark and bleak-looking on the slopes. In the morning cold the train steamed at the platform, the smoke rolling out of the engine stove in great billowing drafts. The steam cloud licked the depot doors, obscuring the people inside and dissolving in gray wisps in the winter air. Gradually passengers emerged one by one from the mist. They set their luggage on the platform to be loaded then found the steps of the car and boarded the train.

Inside the station Mr. Wilkinson stepped up to the counter. He wore the same plain gray hat and suit under a long dark coat and carried the scarred valise. He bought a ticket and turned toward the doors. Two plainclothes detectives were stopping people at the platform. He waited until they were talking to someone, then he walked right past them. He stepped through the doors onto the platform and climbed onto the train, disappearing from view.

David sat waiting in a chair by the bed. Bleak light shone coldly through the window, slanting across the blankets covering her thin figure. He blinked in the pale morning. Everything was still. The room smelled of disinfectant.

The doctor had been gone for hours. He'd said there was nothing else he could do and had been afraid to move her to the hospital. They had swaddled the child in a blanket and laid her in a tiny carved mahogany box. Sarah had gone to bed an hour earlier and was asleep in another room. David had not slept or eaten.

He rubbed his face and blinked again to stay awake. He watched her there in the bed. For the first time her body shifted. He watched her. She breathed deeply and moved her hand over the blanket. Her skin was so pale. Her eyelids fluttered. She moved again and slowly woke. He got down out of the chair and knelt beside her and held her hand. She opened her eyes and stared up into the room. She looked at him. For a moment it was all right. Then she remembered.

Her voice was just a whisper. "Where's my baby?"

He looked at her and he couldn't say anything. His face went to pieces and he had to look away.

"I'm sorry," he said softly. "I'm so sorry."

She turned her face away from him and sank back into the bed and closed her eyes.

They came into the room to get him. He didn't look up when the door opened. They stood there in the doorway while another one brought in a wheelchair. His mouth was dry. He was very thirsty. His eyes were open but he just stared straight ahead at nothing.

They lifted him into the wheelchair and brought him down the hall into a room where their voices echoed against the tiles. There was the sterile smell of bleach. They left him there and a woman came in and ran water into a basin. He sat there quiet, breathing in the steam. The water sounded hollow in the bare white room.

She undressed him and washed his face and body with a warm cloth. She lathered his jaw and shaved him and rinsed the soap away. She rubbed something into his bare scalp. She rinsed him again and dried him and helped him into a clean shirt. He didn't say anything, not looking at her, just staring ahead vacant and passive in the silence.

Dr. Perry came out of the bedroom and David was waiting in the hall. The doctor looked at him and he knew how bad it was. Standing there in shirtsleeves with his bag in the shadowed hall the doctor seemed tired and old. David tried to say something but couldn't.

"She's lost so much blood," the doctor said. "I just don't know—"

"I don't want her to have any more pain."

"I already gave her a quarter grain of morphine. I'd be afraid to give her any more."

"Would it do any good to get her to the hospital?"

"No," the doctor said. "I don't think so. I don't want to move her right now and there's nothing more they could do there either."

David looked at him.

"I want to be with her," he said.

"All right. Go on."

He went into the room and stood there looking at her. Her face was drawn and ash gray. He went over to the bed and knelt down and took her hand. She was very still. Her eyes were hooded slits. Her breath came slow and deliberate. She looked at him. Her voice sounded distant and small.

"It hurts," she said.

"I know, baby—"

"Oh, it hurts."

She inhaled once, more deeply this time. She didn't speak anymore.

He put his head down on her hand and closed his eyes. He kissed her hand again and again, listening to the faint, labored rasp of her lungs. He watched her. After a moment she gasped silently once, and then Angeline took her last breath and died. She lay there pale and still, her eyes and mouth open.

He held her hand and kissed it and pressed it hard against his forehead and he wept.

"Oh no," he said softly. "Oh no."

38

Only a few people attended the funeral. They stood waiting in front of the church steps dressed in black in the raw bleak morning. Angeline's sister was there from Montgomery with her husband. They came in first and sat very still and quiet near the front, staring ahead over the empty pews.

I said a Mass and a brief prayer. The organ played and I stepped down out of the pulpit. The pallbearers came up the steps and lifted the coffin and went back down the aisle toward the doors. The mourners rose and filed out of the pews behind them. The open doors were a patch of flat ashen light at the end of a dark tunnel.

Outside they lifted the casket into truck bed. A man followed us out carrying the tiny dark box that held the child. The day was damp and cold. The wind bit into us as we walked down the frozen road to the graveyard. A thin dirty veil of snow shrouded the ground.

A patch of snow had been cleared away and the grave waited there. Down the sides of the pit I could see where the ground was frozen at the surface and dark and wet as it went deeper. A few feet away gaped a second hole, smaller and narrower. A mound of dark backfill lay heaped and waiting. The gravedigger stood at a distance, watching blankly. A cloth was spread out on the damp ground and the casket lay there and beside it the small coffin of the infant.

David stood looking into the open grave. His face was drawn and exhausted. The men came up to the edge and lowered the box down on ropes. When they finished they pulled up the rigging and stepped back. David came up to the hole. They gave him the spade and he leaned and dug into the mound and let the first dark soil fall over the box. Then he gave back the shovel and stepped away and stood watching them fill the grave.

When they'd finished a few people came up to him and said how sorry they were. He shook their hands absently and looked away at the dark line of trees along the river.

The lights were turned off in the ward and the big windows along the wall admitted regions of bleak winter light, fading into shadow in the corners and along the high ceiling. He sat in a chair by the windows and smoked and stared out. He could hear someone coming down the hall. The doctor came in and sat down in a chair across from him. He held a clipboard on his lap. The doctor studied him a moment.

"How do you feel?"

He took a drag from his cigarette and stared off. His voice sounded flat when he spoke.

"I feel all right," he said. "Tired is all."

The doctor wrote on the clipboard and looked at him again.

"Do you have any plans?"

He looked at the man but didn't answer.

"What are you going to do now?"

He frowned and looked away. He didn't say anything for a moment.

"Go home, I guess."

The doctor nodded and wrote again. The pen scratched against the paper. Daniel looked up into the corners of the ceiling.

"Are there flies in here?"

The doctor stopped writing and looked at him.

"Flies?"

"I hear flies," he said. "Buzzing."

In the weak morning sun hoarfrost whitened the hollow. The sound of a car engine came low and faint around the mountain. The Ford appeared along the dirt road, black and sleek through the bare stark trees. The car pulled past the vacant guard post and rolled down the hill into the clearing. It slowed and pulled up in the gravel and the engine died.

David got out of the car. He wore a black overcoat. He stood in the gravel and looked. Splinters of glass were scattered everywhere through the camp. The company house was a smoking wreck. Jagged remnants of its stone foundations jutted up out of the ground. A few men were picking through the ashes, stepping around patches that were still hot. Burnt beams lay black and scaly in the debris. The soot-stained brick chimney stood in the ruin. In the waste he could see the dark smoldering cube of the iron safe that had sat in the corner of his office. They saw the car parked down in the camp and waved to him. He started walking up the hill.

◆ ◆ ◆

He walked slow and deliberate down the corridor. The orderly stayed close beside him to keep him steady. He looked down the hall at the patch of sky in the front windows. He blinked in the light reflecting off the polished tile floor of the lobby. He had his own clothes on. One of the nurses had given him an old dark overcoat to wear. When they emerged from the corridor the orderly stopped him and said something to the woman at the desk, then turned and disappeared back down the hall.

The woman laid out some papers and slid a pen forward on the oak counter. He stood there looking down at the forms. The woman watched him from behind the counter. He frowned, and after a moment took the pen. He scratched his signature on the paper. He put the pen down and without looking back turned and walked out of the lobby. He passed through the doors into the winter morning and down the steps to the car waiting there to take him away.

39

In the afternoon I walked outside and stood in the churchyard. The mourners were long gone and the gravel lot deserted by the road. Down through the bare trees I could see the river, low and dark in its bed. The whole valley was quiet. I stood for a moment and listened to the river and the winter stillness.

The mountains loomed white with rime and above them the sky stretched flat and ashen, the world utterly void of color. At that moment I was unable to feel any sorrow or loss. Looking out over the barren landscape I only felt tired, and the desire for shelter and some relief from my numbness.

I walked to the church and climbed the steps onto the porch between the columns and pushed in the door. I stood in the dark doorway waiting for some reason or sign. I barely had the heart to go inside. The wind came up across the field and blew the spindly black branches against the church. I felt the chill and stepped inside and closed the door against the cold.

He stood in the doorway of the shack. The door hung open off its hinges as if some animal had pushed it in. His breath smoked in the cold air. He stood there on the threshold for a moment and looked inside. Weak light fell at his back, casting an ambiguous shadow into the room.

The wind blew in the door and a few dead leaves scuttered over the floorboards. The table and chair lay overturned, the mattress pulled halfway onto the floor. He stepped inside and stood in the middle of the room. He looked around the ruined cabin. The air stank of animal scat and urine. He walked over to the old battered desk in the corner of the room and pulled open the drawer.

I stood at the altar rail and stared absently back into the shadowed apse at the niches along the curve of the domed room. I don't know how long I stood there. After a while I felt the door open, the weak light stretching along the benches and a draft of cold air coming into the room. I turned to see who was there.

A man in a dark coat stood in the doorway. With his back against the light I didn't recognize him at first. He stepped deeper into the room and I saw that it was David. He walked down the aisle toward me. I waited there watching him. He came close and his face passed through the light, pale and unshaven. He looked as if he still had not slept.

"Why don't you go on home and get some rest," I said.

He made no response. He came around and sat on the first bench and looked back into the apse. I went over and settled on the bench next to him. We sat together for a long moment without speaking. He stared up along the wall at the panels of stained glass. I sat and watched him. Finally bowed his head and spoke.

"Forgive me, Father, for I have sinned—"

His stopped and his voice fell away into the silence of the room. There was a long pause. I felt some terrible weight pressing down on us. I didn't want him to go on any further. The sound of his voice made me afraid of what he might say. Everything was still. When he spoke again his voice came thick in his throat.

"Sometimes when you love a woman," he said, "she becomes a light, like a sun, and all the beauty and all the meaning in the world seem to shine out of her."

He lifted his head and stared back beyond the altar into the gloom.

"And when you don't have her, you're left alone in the darkness with your own miserable self, and you'll do anything to see that light again and feel it shine on your face."

He turned and looked at me. His eyes were full and glistening. He tried to smile.

"I loved her that way," he said. "When I was with her I could almost feel the secret of it all."

He shook his head. Then he raised up and looked straight at me.

"I killed a man and took his wife," he said.

He stopped and looked down and there was a choking sound in his throat. He sat very still. When it came again his voice was quiet and small, almost a whisper.

"There's nothing now," he said faintly.

I couldn't speak. For a moment I thought the roof might come down and crush us both, but there was no sound, no movement. We both kept perfectly still. I felt a wave of desolation and pity, for him and for all of us.

After a long time I reached over and touched his shoulder. We got up silently and went out of the church and walked down past the graveyard toward the river. In the cold bleak morning he told me everything that had happened and this story formed in my brain.

An hour later we walked back up the hill from the bank. We shook hands and said goodbye. He told me he would come and see me again. He walked out to his car and got in behind the wheel and turned the engine and looked back at me as he pulled away. I stood in the empty churchyard and watched him disappear down the road.

The car pulled up in the frozen gravel and stopped. David got out and stood in the drive. The house stood hard and stark in the winter afternoon. The sky was opaque, bone-colored behind the mountains. The field veiled in thin snow, the woods beyond barren and desolate. He came up the walk and climbed the steps onto the porch and entered the house.

He closed the door behind him and stood in the shadow of the front hall. His breath steamed faintly in the air. He listened back into the house. No sound. No movement. He took off his coat and hung it in the hall closet and went up the stairs.

He stood in the doorway and looked into the empty bedroom. The window had been left open and the cold air was coming in but he did not move to close the window. He sat down on the edge of the bed. For a long time he sat and stared into the silence.

From somewhere outside he heard an unfamiliar voice call.

"Who's home?"

The words echoed out across the field, hollow and cold. He went to the window and looked out over the bleak landscape. He did not see anyone. He scanned the trees at the bottom of the hill. A man stood at the edge of the woods. He wore a dark coat. David stared for a long moment but did not know him. He went to the closet and found the shotgun and went out of the bedroom and down the stairs.

He came out and stood on the porch with the door open behind him and looked out across the field. The man stood at the edge of the trees. David came down the steps and started walking out into the thin snow with the shotgun. The dead garden stretched out in the field like a dry brown scab on the ground. Pale wisps of snow in the corn stubble. The man stood very still, watching him come.

David stopped in the snow. He held the shotgun on the man and looked at him. He was clean shaven, his head shorn almost bald. Dark stubble shadowed his skull. His eyes black, his face pale and emaciated. He seemed frail and old, though his age was hard to tell. He stared ahead, his face blank, impassive. Nothing showed in his look, the way he held his mouth. Only his eyes hinted at some remote, inaccessible sorrow.

David studied him.

"Do I know you?"

The man didn't answer. He just stood there, staring blankly. David looked down and saw the pistol held loosely in the sleeve of his ragged coat. He looked again at his face. Then he knew him.

David raised the shotgun barrel and held it on him. Daniel made no movement, staring ahead with the same vacant look. David stood before him. The black steel barrel of the shotgun against the snow, the pale bloom of his breath in the still air.

Daniel seemed to gaze past him, somewhere off into the bleak distance at nothing. Then a shadow of anguish and profound sadness passed over his face. As if he were sorry for them both, as if compelled to do some terrible thing unwilled.

David slowly lowered the shotgun and made as if to speak. The younger man seemed to come back. He looked at David. He raised the pistol absently. For a moment David regarded the gun pointed at him. Its dull cast, its coal black skin. He stood very still. Then he breathed in and closed his eyes. On his face a look that seemed resigned, almost calm.

The pistol cracked in the silence. Its noise reechoed in the void. The shotgun slipped away as he fell. The wound bloomed like a huge red flower out of his forehead, an enormous blood-colored rose. He lay very still. The red was a spreading stain in the snow around his shoulders. At that moment all the pain passed out of his face and he looked placid, as if he wondered at some unknowable question.

Daniel stared down at him for a moment, his face pallid and blank. Then he raised the pistol to his temple and pulled the trigger.

40

A shovel breaks the hard ground. It hollows and mounds the split earth in regular time, one measure by one. The gravedigger labors on under the bleak winter sky and the ruined tree stripped of its leaves. His digging is steady and rhythmic, never halting, never faltering.

I stand under the bare branches among the blasted roots, hunting shelter out of the wind in vain. I look on in the silence as he works, breath smoking gray in the slanting gray light.

Now only the mountains show some faint hint that in time winter will end. Soon the first wet tips of buds will push themselves out of the boughs into a world reborn. Beyond the hill the columned graves stretch out now in the barren field along the cold, muddy bank. In spring long grass will grow again over the mounds that the reverend dead leave in the earth, covering them completely.

In this world even the most beautiful person there is was born to die. They light it up, they shine, and their voices are the music that the rest of us dream by. And when they go down to grief and the gods below, we keep singing that song to remind us of their great, suffering hearts, and the brief hour of beauty that left us in their grace.

978-0-595-44173-0
0-595-44173-4

Made in the USA
Lexington, KY
06 March 2012